He seemed to know everything about them, and he was using his knowledge to terrify them...

Michael jumped up and looked around. The kidnapper had his back to Abby as he lifted the cover off the box. Michael began to scream. Abby couldn't see what the kidnapper was holding until he turned round and walked toward her. Then she saw the glass box full of tarantulas.

He put the box down in front of her and then he inserted a key in the roof of her cage. She hadn't seen the lock since it was obscured by the wooden structure surrounding the toilet at the back. It opened a large panel of glass.

He opened the lid of the box and tipped the tarantulas into Abby's cage. He began filming it on his mobile phone. The tarantulas fell on top of each other, crawling across one another's backs, their bellies bloated as they scuttled across the glass floor. Abby inched away and pressed her back against the front of her cage.

"I know you're not afraid of spiders. It's snakes that make you terrified, Abby," the kidnapper said, his voice metallic, and devoid of intonation.

She turned round and tried to see into his eyes. "You said you'd only do this if you weren't paid."

"I haven't been paid."

"What do you want from us?"

"I want you to know what it feels like to be made of glass."

Therapy cured them of their phobias, but in the glass house, the kidnapper is taking the cure away…

When the adult children of two wealthy families are kidnapped, private detective Earl Blake enters a labyrinth of lies and evasions as he attempts to rescue them. The kidnapper wants money the families can't come up with, and Earl finds himself in a race against time to find Michael and Abby before it is too late.

KUDOS for *Locked in Cages*

"I find Richard Godwin to be an exceptional writer with an extraordinarily fine mind. He conducted over two weeks the single best interview I've ever been involved with. His novels are always good, with crackling dialogue. His latest, *Wrong Crowd*, is dazzling. Read him."
~ Luke Rhinehart, author of the bestselling *The Dice Man*, the novel that inspired Sir Richard Branson to found the Virgin Empire.

"A psychological mystery by a master of his craft." ~ Matt Hilton, author of the *Joe Hunter* thrillers

"Set in England, the story is well-written, and the action is fast and intense. This one will keep you reading all the way through." ~ *Taylor Jones, Reviewer*

"*Locked in Cages* is a fast-paced, complex thriller that will have you biting your nails and turning pages as fast as you can." ~ *Regan Murphy, Reviewer*

LOCKED IN CAGES

RICHARD GODWIN

A Black Opal Books Publication

GENRE: PSYCHOLOGICAL THRILLER/MYSTERY-DETECTIVE

LOCKED IN CAGED
Copyright © 2016 by Richard Godwin
Cover Design by Page Godwin
All cover art copyright © 2016
All Rights Reserved
Print ISBN: 978-1-626945-84-5

First Publication: DECEMBER 2016

Published by Black Opal Books **http://www.blackopalbooks.com**

DEDICATION

For Paris Tongue

CHAPTER 1

It was Samantha Villa who hired Earl Blake, much to her husband Julian's annoyance.

"You're really going to entrust our son's welfare to that man?" he said.

"I know you don't like me seeing my exes, but he's the best."

"The best at what?"

"Finding people."

"Or is it an excuse to see him? Mr. Rugged?"

"Guilty talk, Julian, your tic has returned."

Julian Villa stood glaring at her in his Armani suit, clutching a glass of whiskey, as the doorbell rang. He put the glass down, smoothed his eyebrows with his thumbs, and ran his hand through his thick black hair. He was a handsome man with a tanned face—a picture of health, whose manners seemed to hide a feral instinct. He adjusted his gold tie, nudging it farther into his sheer white collar.

"That must be him," Julian said, "your private investigator, although why you chose him when I have a list of the best in the business leads me to some interesting questions."

"He *is* the best in the business. Are you going to let him in?"

"I hope he wipes his feet on the mat of our beautiful home."

"A house is not a home, Julian."

Samantha went downstairs as Julian composed himself in the living room of their Kensington house. She fussed with her hair in the mirror in the marble tiled hall. It was blonde and lustrous and caressed her shoulders. Samantha was in her early forties and had a face that all men looked at twice. It was both beautiful and reserved in a way that gave her instant mystique, and her skin was as supple as that of a woman in her twenties. She had unearthly blue eyes, as clear as polished lapis. They took you in and gently drifted from your face, as if she were lost in some inner sadness. Her hands were shaking as she opened the door.

Earl was standing there with his motorcycle helmet in one hand, that same sparkle in his deep green eyes that made her high all those years ago. She looked away from him and at his bike, parked neatly before their immaculate lawn. And she realised the despair she'd felt for days was fading. She wanted to reach out and touch Earl's face, she wanted to think forbidden things. But Julian was upstairs and the burden of her marriage weighed on her, as if he was standing behind her, laying a heavy hand on her shoulder.

"New bike?" she said, annoyed at herself for the trite question.

He nodded.

"Looks fast. You always did like fast bikes, Earl."

"Kawasaki Ninja."

"Come in."

The brevity of his responses unnerved her, and she wondered if it was a mistake calling him over the abduction. But Earl had kept his intelligent, masculine gaze on her from the moment she opened the door, and Samantha felt scrutinised in a way that was not unpleasant. He stepped into the hall and looked at the large staircase and the oak panels on the first landing.

"Nice place, it's been a few years, Sam, but you haven't changed."

"I'll take that as a compliment," she said, offering him her cheek and feeling like a teenager again.

"You said you need me to find someone."

"Our son's been abducted. You better come upstairs and meet Julian."

She wondered if she'd overdressed for a meeting that

was meant to be business-like and dignified with pain, and although she was in pain, she glanced at her pearl earrings in the mirror over the sofa as she walked into the living room and recalled an argument long ago with Earl about her taste in jewellery. He'd accused her of being lavish in the days before the money came along, and she wondered now what he felt about her. She looked over at Julian. He had his back to them and was looking out of the window. He turned and gave Earl his best smile, the perfect fake that Samantha knew so well.

"Earl, so nice to see you after all these years," he said, striding across the parquet floor and shaking Earl's hand warmly. "I'm sorry our reunion has been brought about by such sad news. I'm sure my wife has told you the reason for her contacting you. I also hear you're adept at finding missing people."

"I've worked on a few cases."

"It's our son, Michael, you see."

"Samantha tells me he's been abducted."

"Indeed."

"Have you had communication from his kidnapper?"

"We have, and it's of a most unpleasant and disturbing kind."

"We got a film in the post yesterday, that's when I couldn't take it anymore," Samantha said.

"Can I see it?"

"Of course. Forgive me, I haven't offered you a drink," Julian said.

"Thank you, I'll have a club soda."

Julian went over to the bar, took a can out of the fridge, and poured it into a glass, adding a slice of lemon with a pair of silver tongs. "Let's go next door," he said, handing Earl the glass.

Earl followed him and Samantha into a room that overlooked the back gardens and a large fountain. The room was ornately decorated with rich blue and red velvets. A huge plasma screen occupied an entire wall. Julian went over to a mahogany cabinet and opened it. Inside was a large collection of DVDs. He removed one and put it into the player.

"This is shocking," Samantha said.

They all stood as the film played.

The first shot was of two glass cages in a bare room without windows. Earl estimated the cages were about eight foot cubed. Inside one was a young man who was pacing the enclosure. In the other a young woman sat on the floor with her knees up against her chest and her head pressed against them, hiding her face. The cages each contained a section at the rear that was boarded off with what looked like plywood. It was impossible to see behind it. The cages faced each other. The camera zoomed in on each cage, pausing at the man's face, then the woman's as she looked up and began to cry. Then the film stopped.

Julian hit the remote control, sending the screen into darkness.

"That was Michael in the cage?" Earl said.

Samantha dabbed her eyes with a tissue. "Yes, and the young woman is Abby Sheen."

"You know her?"

"She and Michael have known each other for years."

"She's the daughter of friends of ours, Greg and Felicity," Julian said.

"When did they go missing?"

Julian fiddled with his right cuff link, his eyes on the Persian rug. "Two days ago."

"And that's all you've received?"

"I had a phone call the day before the film arrived."

"Saying what?"

"It was a man's voice, one I don't recognise. He said, 'I have your son and his little friend. I'm taking them to the glass house where they will remain until you pay me two million pounds. If you involve the police I will kill them both, you will never find their remains. Do not throw any stones, or you will shatter everything you hold dear.'"

"Did you trace the call?"

"I tried to, it came through on my mobile, but it was made using Skype."

"So, it's Thursday today, you received the call on Tuesday?"

"Yes."

"You got the film yesterday?"

"Right."

"Have you contacted the police?"

"No. I want to see my son alive again."

"Who did you use to try to trace the call?"

"I have people I use for security. They're better than British Telecom."

"Can either of you think of anyone who would want to harm Michael or Abby?"

"No. This is about money, right?"

"It is. But I think it's more than that." Earl sipped his soda and glanced at Samantha. She looked diminished, her beauty paler than a few moments before, as if a worm had slipped inside her and was eating at her heart.

"More how?" Julian said.

"What is the glass house?"

"I don't know."

"This is a very specific way of keeping people prisoner. He could have locked them in separate rooms. He's got them under observation. Have you thought of paying him?"

"Isn't that a mistake? I read that was a sure way to lose your child."

"It depends whether they've seen his face. Many kidnappers do let their hostages go once they've been paid, but they make sure they can't be identified."

"But if we pay him what then?" Samantha said.

"It depends what his terms of payment are. If he wants cash, we could arrange for him to bring Michael and Abby with him when I drop the money off."

"But then we'd see him."

"He'd hide his face."

"And what if he wants a bank wire?" Julian said.

"That's harder, but more unlikely because he could be traced."

Samantha put her hand on Earl's. "I just want Michael out of there, please help us."

Earl could feel Julian's eyes burning his skin. "I'll do everything I can."

"He's a vulnerable young man, he's had troubles, you know," she said.

"Can you tell me a bit about that?"

"He found it hard to adapt. He hasn't really had a job, but he tried working for his father. He had therapy for his problems."

"What were they?"

"Nightmares, terrible nightmares since he was a boy. He was always tired because he'd be awake all night. I used to hear him screaming."

"What were the nightmares?"

"Always the same. Spiders, Michael used to dream tarantulas were crawling all over him. He'd wake up and check every inch of his room at night with a torch. He hated them. He couldn't touch a spider, even a tiny one. He bought a lizard for a pet. He told me he thought a spider had crawled inside his ear at night and was eating his brain. That's when he went into therapy."

"Did it help?"

"No, it made it worse," Julian said. "If you ask me, these therapists are a bunch of nutters."

"You think?"

"Self-serving charlatans with a theory to peddle which they do at others' expense. They care nothing for others' welfare. No, what did help was hiring a hypno-therapist. He got rid of the phobia. In fact, Michael had begun to be a normal young man again, enjoying the kinds of things young men should."

"And now this happens," Samantha said.

"The more information I get the better. I need to get a picture of Michael and Abby."

"How is this connected to his abduction?" Julian said.

"It gives me an insight into your son's character. The kidnapper either knows him or Abby or one of you or Abby's parents in some way, even if he's read about you in the paper. But if this was a straightforward case of you being targeted because of your wealth, your son wouldn't be locked in a glass cage."

"So you think this is more personal."

"I do."

Julian looked at his watch. "How much do you charge?"

"Four hundred a day, plus expenses."

"Do you need me to sign an agreement?"

"That won't be necessary."

Julian turned his back and stared out of the window.

"Thank you, Earl," Samantha said.

"How old is Michael?"

"Twenty-four."

"And Abby?"

"Twenty-two," Samantha said.

"I need to talk to her parents."

"I'll call them. They're quite desperate as we are. I spoke to them last night and mentioned you. Julian and I thought it would be best if we met you on our own, in case you didn't take it on."

"Has the kidnapper contacted either of them?"

"They've received the film," Julian said, turning round. "Greg got a call on his mobile. It was the same message applied to Abby."

"He's asking for another two million?"

"That's right. I tried tracing the call, but came up with the same result."

"Is there anyone you may have offended in your business dealings?"

"No, what I do is above board."

"Offenses can sometimes be caused by things we wouldn't ever consider."

"I can't imagine this has anything to do with business."

"You're a wealthy man, Julian, you're described as a real estate magnate."

"You said if this was just about money, my son, wouldn't be held in a glass cage."

"This kidnapper wants money. He's also trying to convey a specific point."

"What?"

"That I don't know yet."

CHAPTER 2

Earl left at one p.m. The row began immediately, but he didn't hear it. The noise of his Ninja drowned it out as he rode away. Julian and Samantha were yelling as Earl meandered through the lunchtime traffic to his newly appointed apartment in Hammersmith. He lived just behind the stretch of Thames that drifted past The Blue Anchor, all the way to The Dove, his favorite drinking spot on quiet weekends, when the local families had gone away on their summer holidays, and that corner of London reminded him of how it used to be when he rowed nearby.

Earl took the stairs to his apartment on the top floor of the building, removed his leathers, and made some lunch. As Earl watched the Thames curl like a snake into the distance, Julian was pouring himself another whisky while Samantha tried to forget the image of her son locked in a glass cage.

Julian had started shouting at her when he found her gazing after Earl through the living room window as he got on his bike. She was looking at his athletic physique, recalling how he used to make love to her all those years ago—and all the things she gave to him when she was young and had them to give—wondering if it was his memory that had been the pain in her heart all these years.

"If you're going to have an affair, make it less obvious," Julian said.

Samantha turned round as she heard the Kawasaki's engine rev outside. Her heart was racing, and she couldn't tell whether it was excitement or anxiety she was feeling. "Don't you take the moral high ground, Julian," she said. "You're the adulterer in this marriage."

"It was eighteen years ago."

"So you say. But someone forgot to tell me."

"Oh, why don't you drop it? I've given you everything, you ungrateful bitch."

"You really believe that?"

"Look at this, you live in an eight-bedroom, six-bathroom house in Kensington, you have cleaners every day, you don't have to do anything." A red vein throbbed at the corner of his face. His tic twitched at his right eye as he followed Samantha around the room. "I fly you in private Lear jets on holidays when I work—stop walking away from me."

"You jet me away so you can fuck one of your mistresses. Do you bring them here?"

"I don't have mistresses."

"Do you pay the maids to clean up your stains? You're good at that, paying people to do your dirty deeds."

"What is that supposed to mean?"

"What do you think it means? Julian Villa always looks so respectable, but his wife knows the real man."

The laugh he produced looked like a scar breaking across his face. There was no mirth in it, his eyes were cold, and behind the smile, his intensely white teeth looked like chiseled stones against his lips.

"You're lucky," he said, sipping from his cut glass.

"Am I? Do explain that, Julian. Perhaps I'm a bit dumb. I must be to be married to you."

"Look at what you have," he said and gestured at the room with his right hand.

"It's a nice house, it's a shame about the company."

"Would you really want to live in a flat in Hammersmith?"

"How do you know where Earl lives? You checked him out?"

"There's a lot I know that you don't."

"Yes, so I discovered not so long ago."

"Samantha, I knew your price when I married you. A

man like Earl may be good as a private dick but he's no husband."

"Interesting choice of words. It's almost as if you're tempting me to do it."

"You made your choices when you married me."

"If I did it, it would be in private. You know all about keeping things secret, Julian."

"We were happily married until a few months ago."

"Yes, but I didn't know you'd been fucking my friend."

Julian put his glass down on a Regency table. The gesture was deliberate and self-conscious, as if he was reining in his anger. "It happened once, a long time ago. It was a drunken mistake, which I regret, and it's been blown out of all proportion by those bloody therapists."

"So you keep saying."

"Why don't we concentrate on getting our son back?" he said. "I hope he's up to that."

"There's a lot he's up to."

"And what does that mean?"

"You can see how fit he is, always was. He was in the army. He knows how to fight, but he's also gentle."

"Spare me the details of your sexual past."

"You mean like you did with me, Julian?"

"It was an isolated incident in our marriage. I had no relationship with her, unlike you and Earl."

"I said I'd call the Sheens so Earl can meet them. I'll do that now."

"You'll feel differently when Michael's back."

"Julian, don't get me wrong. There's nothing I want more right now than to know that Michael is safe. But it won't change what I feel about you after your infidelity."

"Give it time."

"You mean eighteen years?"

"You better make that call."

"Julian, who has our son?"

"I've no idea, but let's hope Mr. Rugged lives up to his reputation and finds him fast."

CHAPTER 3

At four p.m. that afternoon Earl parked the Ninja outside the Sheen's seven-bedroom Georgian Villa that gazed out at Richmond Green. The shine on the front door was so clear he could see his own refection in it as he rang the bell. An extremely beautiful woman opened it. Earl's mind was torn between two things about her in the few seconds as he waited for her to speak. Her facial structure and thick dark hair were breath taking, but there was a deep unhappiness in her eyes, and her clothes were chosen without effort—colorless slacks with creases, an old cardigan with holes in the sleeves that looked as though moths had eaten into the wool. She seemed in conflict with her appeal.

"You're Earl," she said, with no emphasis, as if she was telling him rather than asking.

"Mrs. Sheen?"

"Please call me Felicity."

She held out her hand. Her fingers were cold and the bones beneath her skin felt as light bird's feathers.

"I'm sure this is a hard time for you and your husband," Earl said, as she stepped aside and he walked into the hall.

She touched the shoulder of his leather jacket.

"If you only knew."

He could smell wine on her breath. She stood there, looking up at him with her mouth slightly open, then she turned and he followed her along the hall to a study.

"This is my husband," she said.

Greg Sheen was putting the phone down as they walked in. He rose from his chair, came round the desk, and shook Earl's hand warmly. "I am so pleased you're taking this on. Samantha speaks highly of you, Mr. Blake."

"Please, Earl is fine."

"Can I offer you a drink?"

"Just a coffee."

"Milk? Sugar?"

"Black."

"Felicity."

"I'd just made some," she said, leaving the room.

Greg Sheen was a tall, well-built man, who looked like a country squire with his ruddy complexion.

"Please, do sit down," he said, motioning to a sofa in the corner of the room.

"The Villas don't have any idea what the kidnapping is about. Do you?"

"None whatsoever. I'm baffled and worried sick. Felicity is ill with anxiety. She has fragile nerves you know. I haven't slept for two nights."

"That's understandable."

"I fear for my daughter. I hope this man's not a pervert."

"Most kidnappings are about money."

"Of course."

"But not all," Felicity said, as she came in with a tray on which sat a cafetiere and a white porcelain cup and saucer.

"No, not all," Earl said.

She nodded and lifted the cafetiere, filling the room with the smell of coffee that had a note of dark chocolate as she poured into his cup.

"You've seen the horrendous film?" she said.

"I have."

"We were sent one, too."

"Is it identical?"

"Well, I don't know. We haven't compared them."

"Do you mind if I look?" Earl said.

Greg opened a cabinet at the far side of the room. Inside it was a TV monitor and a DVD player. He opened a drawer, removed a DVD, and put it in. Greg watched, standing, with his arms folded.

Earl noticed Felicity's eyes were on the faded carpet

as it ended. She'd knitted her fingers together and her knuckles were white.

"Both films are identical," Earl said.

"What does this man want?" Felicity said. "Why is my child being held in glass?"

CHAPTER 4

Leonard Wells dusted fluff off the arm of the tattered sofa in the darkened living room. He could hear a train thundering by at the station. A picture shook on the wall. He got up, straightened it, and stared fondly at the image of his father in his dustman's outfit, smoking a Players—a relic of a past that Leonard felt no longer existed.

Then he left the grimy flat in Kew, passing the Let board that stood outside. He walked two blocks and got on the 485 bus to the hospital. Leonard was unaware of the other passengers until a man in a pin-striped suit got on after a few stops. There were no seats left and he stood reading the *Financial Times*, occasionally bumping Leonard's knee with his leg when the bus turned a corner.

Leonard looked up at him, but the man neither acknowledged the intrusion on his personal space nor offered any apology.

Leonard got off and walked to Kingston Hospital. He went into the shop, bought a bunch of flowers, then took the lift to his mother's ward.

Mary Wells was lying propped up in bed reading a copy of the *Daily Express*. She folded it neatly when she saw her son enter. He laid the flowers on the night table and drew up a chair.

"Those for me, Len?"

"Course."

She gazed at the roses. "You're a good lad."

"So how's it all feeling?"

"Doctor said I should be fit to go home tomorrow."

"That's good."

"How's the sale going?"

"I've rented out the flat. I went there today. I haven't slept there for weeks. I'll go back one more time and get a few things, all your stuff's packed up."

"I want to see your new house, Len."

"You will. I'm doing some work on it."

"I think it's amazing you made all that money. After you got out of the army, I thought you wouldn't work again."

"You know me. I ain't a shirker, Mum."

"Whoever said you were? You were one of the brightest lads in your year, got top grades in class, remember?"

"Course I remember."

"What's the matter, Len?"

"Nothing."

"Still think about it, don't you?"

"Yeah. I dreamed about Kenny last night. It was awful, Mum. There are things I've never spoken about. He was my best mate, and they let us down. All those posh officers don't want to fight, not like us. They cover things up and lie about it. I'll never forget the look in Kenny's eyes. His guts were hanging out. They looked like bleeding eels."

"Please, Len, not in here. Can I have some water?"

An old woman at the next bed tutted and looked away, past the mother and son, out through the grimy window to the polluted gray sky and the hint of a crane in the distance, poised above a building, readying itself for demolition, the only images of an outside world in the sterilized ward.

Mary Wells was in her seventies, with gray hair that looked like steel, sharp blue eyes that sparkled from her small face as she spoke. She had a bird-like body, with little hands that seemed to peck at things rather than clutch them. Leonard loomed down over her as he stood and poured her some water. He was six foot two, and well built. He'd served in Afghanistan, and his years in the army had left him with one habit he refused to shed in a lifestyle he recognized less and less as his own. Leonard kept himself extremely physically fit, working out with weights for several hours a day and running eight miles each morning in the deserted streets, seen only by insomniacs and night workers. Sleep had become a stranger about whom he fantasised in the way some men dreamed of women. He would lie awake, think of how fragmented his life had become, and rise to test his body. He'd once led an ordered military existence. His physical regime was the only constant now. Leonard felt his life was fading from him.

His face was neither handsome nor ugly, but existed somewhere in between. He had intense deep-set eyes, dull brown hair, a curved nose, and a scar on his chin from where a fellow soldier had hit him with a beer bottle in a fight over a girl, before Leonard broke both his arms.

"I was thinking about Dad," he said.

"It doesn't do to dwell on what happened, Len," Mary said, setting the glass down on the night table and glancing at a nurse who had wandered into the ward.

"He worked hard all his life doing a job the snobs in this country turn down their noses at, and look at how he died."

"I don't want to think about it."

"Yeah, well I can't help it. She the one?" he said, glancing in the direction of the nurse.

Mary nodded.

She was a young nurse, in her twenties. She was full-figured and had a pretty face with cold eyes and a down-turned mouth that gave her a sour expression, as if she disdained the work. Her blonde hair was scraped back on her scalp. Leonard noticed her strong calves as she bent to check the notes on the next bed.

"I'm gonna have a word," he said.

"Len."

He stood up and went over to the nurse, who put the notes down and walked away, ignoring him.

"Excuse me," he said.

She stopped and turned.

"I'm not happy about something that took place here a few days ago," Leonard said.

"Can it wait? I'm busy."

"You're busy? How about making sure my mother doesn't die of thirst in here?"

"Is that your mother?"

"Yes."

"She looks all right to me."

"She is now, but you made her wait for hours for a glass of water."

"We're understaffed."

"How about dignity?"

"What?"

"Dignity."

"There's water on her table."

"You don't get it, do you?" Leonard said, raising his voice.

"I don't like the way you're talking to me."

"I don't know why you chose nursing, Pam," Leonard said, glancing at her badge, "but it's clear that you're not fit to be working in a hospital."

"I'm calling a doctor."

"Go ahead, I'll complain to him. You don't care about the elderly."

Pam Smythe went into the corridor as Leonard said, "stuck up tart," and sat down. Dr. Francis Truman was standing by the desk chatting to an attractive young Indian nurse, who was laughing as Pam approached.

"She don't care," Leonard said to his mother. "You'll be out of here soon."

"Don't make a fuss, son."

"Someone has to speak up, or they'll walk all over you."

"Here's the doctor."

Francis Truman walked into the ward, placing a pen in his pocket. Pam Smythe followed him.

"Mr. Wells?" Dr. Truman said.

"Yes?"

"I believe you have a complaint."

"I do, as it happens," Leonard said, standing up and walking toward the doctor, who took a step back.

"One of the nurses says you were being aggressive toward her."

"One of the nurses? Pam you mean?"

"There is a sign that states we do not accept abusive behavior of any kind."

"Abusive behavior? What are you talking about?"

"She says you swore at her."

"Well, she's lying then."

Leonard inched toward Dr. Truman. His physical presence began to unnerve the doctor.

"I will have to ask you to refrain from harassing my nurses."

"Yeah, only you can do that."

"What did you say?"

"I seen you, met many like you, and you're all the same. Seen you chatting them up, fancy yourself, don't you? Look down on people like us. Got a wife have you? She know?"

Truman blushed. "I beg your pardon?"

"She know about how you carry on?"

"I am going to ask you to leave."

"How come no one has explained why my mother nearly died of thirst in here?"

"You're going too far."

"She had to wait for hours for a drink."

"It's the first I've heard of this."

"Shows how much interest you pay, don't it?"

"Mr. Wells, please leave, I have patients to attend to."

"Or what?"

"I'll call security."

Leonard moved close enough to breathe the fried egg he'd had for breakfast into the doctor's face. "Do you know what I'd do to your security guys? Any idea?"

"Are you threatening me?"

"Len, don't make trouble, best go now, come again tomorrow, bring me some more flowers," Mary said.

Leonard's gaze was locked on the doctor's face, and it broke as he heard his mother's voice. He turned round, went over to her bed, bent, and kissed her tenderly on the forehead, then walked toward the door. As he passed Pam Smythe, he noticed a smirk on her face. He stopped and looked at her.

"If you do visit your mother tomorrow, you will have to respect our staff," Truman said.

Leonard held out both arms, his palms facing the doctor, who looked at Leonard's empty hands.

"Me? I'm good as gold."

Then he left and went to the toilet in the corridor. A few minutes later he walked up to the desk where Pam Smythe was writing on a clipboard.

"I'll wipe that off your face," he whispered in her ear.

"I'll make sure you don't visit again."

"And I'll make sure of something more. I can imagine you at it with him."

"I'm calling security."

Leonard had left the building by the time they reached his mother's ward. He was walking toward the bus stop, checking his mobile phone. Mary Wells was trying to explain her son to Pam, whose disinterest in her account was unapparent to Mary.

"He's a good lad," Mary said, laying her right hand

on Pam's arm as she readjusted her bed. "He was in the army, saw some terrible things, bit of a war hero."

Mary winked at Pam, who looked away.

"Do you have enough water?" she said.

"Oh, yes."

CHAPTER 5

They were having drinks in the Villas' living room. Julian stood behind Samantha's chair with his right hand on the back as she sipped wine and talked to Greg, who was hunched forward on the sofa. Felicity hovered near a window in a cream satin dress, set apart from the company, as ephemeral as a whisper in the mist. Earl had arrived at seven p.m. and sat on the sofa next to Greg.

"We've got you some photographs of Michael," Julian said, pointing at the coffee table.

There were several pictures of him on its immaculately polished surface. As Earl studied them, he noticed how serious and worried Michael looked.

"We've brought some of Abby," Greg said, handing

him four shots of a pretty woman with a strained smile.

Earl sipped his Courvoisier.

"What have you found out?" Julian said.

"The packages the films were sent in were mailed from a post office in Acton. I went there today and, unfortunately, there are no cameras outside that might have taken a picture of the kidnapper, or whoever posted them. There is a camera in the shop, but I can't get access to its contents."

"So where does that leave us?" Samantha said.

"The police could view the film. We have the time of posting."

"No," Julian said, "I don't want my son killed."

Felicity came forward, clutching her glass of red wine. "Does this man have us under surveillance?"

"That's unlikely," Earl said.

She finished her drink, the drops of wine, like beads of blood, dripping down the inner bell of the glass. One of them hung on her lip.

"Then what do we have to find our children?" she said.

"Money, that's what we have," Julian said.

Samantha stood up and straightened her dress. "Earl, what should we do?"

"He hasn't given you instructions as to how to pay him yet. He'll be in touch."

"But if we pay him he may kill them both," she said.

"I'm not suggesting you do pay him, but to see if we

can find him when he gives his instructions. He'll probably ask for the cash to be dropped off somewhere."

"So you watch him as he picks the money up?" Julian said.

"If possible. If he chooses a drop-off point, I can follow him."

"Why hasn't he asked for the money yet?"

"There could be many reasons," Earl said. "I think he's trying to scare you, get you ready to pay."

"Well, he's succeeding in that," Samantha said. "I keep thinking of the glass house and what it means."

Felicity laid her hand on Earl's arm. She crouched down on her knees and gazed into his face.

"Find Abby, please find her. She's a delicate young woman, easily afraid. God knows what this is doing to her."

"And they'd both done so well with therapy," Samantha said, going over to the bar and pouring herself another glass of Sauvignon Blanc. "Refill, anyone?"

"My glass is empty, like my heart," Felicity said. She ran her right hand through her hair and laughed. "I'm sorry, this business is making me a little crazy."

"A little?" Greg said.

"My husband is a saint, that's why I married him. Greg has always been so patient with me. I'm highly strung, I have strange habits, you know."

She sipped her wine and went over to her husband, who stood and put both hands on her shoulders.

"Earl will find them," he said.

"I need to be weighed down or I'll float away, tie me to the wall and ignore me, please."

Earl looked at them, Julian standing behind Samantha, Greg touching Felicity's shoulders, and they seemed couples set in a tableau that both mystified and unnerved him. There was a bitterness to their mannerisms, and the conversation they were conducting seemed like a fragile veneer beneath which an entirely different dialogue lay.

"You mentioned that Abby had been seeing a therapist," he said.

Felicity's eyes weren't focused. She was lost in a memory or thought that had no place among the gathering. Earl noticed Samantha looking at her in irritation as Julian tapped his index finger on the chair. Greg sat down again, slung his right leg over his left, and began to inspect the laces of his brogues.

Earl had seen it before, the stress on parents when their children were kidnapped. But this crowd seemed to be coming unglued by the minute. Samantha looked angry. Only Julian maintained the same demeanor, as if it was beneath him to show what was going on inside him.

Then Felicity did the strangest thing. She put her glass down, took each of her wrists in the other hand, and, gripping them, tilted her head back. Her breathing was rapid, and she was shaking beneath her satin dress. Her breasts shook beneath the material, and a blue vein ran across her neck, raised from the surface of her skin like the root of a tree that had burst through the soil. Earl thought she was hyperventilating and was about to go over to her. Then she picked up her drink, came over, and sat next to him on the sofa, squeezing in between him and Greg, her thigh touching Earl's.

Samantha glared at her. Felicity leaned forward, her face inches from Earl's. There was a transparency to her skin and her wrists were red from where she'd gripped them.

"The therapy, yes," she said. "Two years of therapy to be exact."

"What was it for?" Earl said.

"Abby had problems. We discovered she snorted."

"Coke?"

Felicity nodded. "She also had a phobia. Most people don't know what a phobia is. They think it's a neurosis or fear, but it's crippling. She had a disability. My girl was so terrified sometimes she couldn't get out of bed or leave the house. She'd become suicidal, irrational."

"What was her phobia?"

"Snakes, Earl, snakes. She saw them everywhere. Shapes assumed serpentine forms to Abby, sober or not. She heard them hiss at night and dreamed they were crawling inside her."

"Both our children were phobic," Samantha said. "Do you think it's significant, Earl?"

"I think it's unusual."

"You must think we're all nuts," Greg said.

"No, I don't think you're all nuts. Kidnapping places people under unbearable pressure."

"Well, while we're all talking about snakes," Julian said, "both our children are in the hands of a man who may be dangerous. We're still no nearer to knowing how to rescue them."

"I can put the post office from where the parcels were sent under surveillance. It's unlikely he'll use it twice, but it's worth a shot. In the meantime, we need to wait for his instructions. The more I know about Abby and Michael, the better. I need to speak to their friends."

"How will that help?"

"If there is a personal reason the kidnapper has chosen them, then I may get a clue as to why. Their friends may have seen someone hanging around. Did Abby have a boyfriend?"

"There's her ex," Felicity said.

"Okay, I'll start with him. Michael?"

"He was seeing a girl, Susy, very sweet. I don't think they're still seeing each other," Samantha said.

"Can I have the names of their therapists?"

"I'll get them for you," Julian said, leaving the room.

"Were either of them studying?"

"Abby was trying," Greg said. "She'd begun an arts course at Richmond University, but she kept skipping lectures."

"And Michael?"

"Julian kept pushing him to," Samantha said, "and

the more he pushed, the worse it got. He'd started a course a few months ago."

"Where was that?"

"Kensington College of Business. He didn't go far, hated it. It was Julian's idea, he wanted his son modeled in his own image."

"I suppose you're telling him what a lousy father I am," Julian said, coming into the room with a piece of paper, which he handed to Earl.

"I'm just describing the kind of relationship you had with Michael," Samantha said.

"Are you?"

Earl looked at the paper on which Julian had written two names and phone numbers in turquoise ink.

"Which therapist was Michael's?"

"Dave Ruby, highly recommended," Julian said.

"Although you think you wasted your money?"

"It's a load of claptrap."

"But it helped your son?"

"That's arguable."

"And Marion Wakefield was Abby's."

"That's right," Greg said.

"Do you think she was good?"

"Hard to say. It's not something I know much about."

"Did Abby seem to benefit from it?"

"Either that or the hypnosis."

"Who were the hypnotists?"

"It was just one," Julia said, "Stuart Parkes. Here, I'll write his name and number down."

He picked his iPhone up from a small table next to him then took the piece of paper Earl had set down on the coffee table and wrote Parkes's number on it.

"I'll get you Susy's number," Samantha said.

"Felicity, perhaps I can speak with Abby's ex?"

"Miguel? I'm sure I can find his number somewhere, but he's at the university, if not."

"In the meantime, let me know if you get another film."

Felicity wrapped her arms around her shoulders. "You mean he'll send more?"

Earl stood up. "It's likely."

"I'll get you that number," Samantha said, coming out into the hall with him.

He waited as she went to the end of the corridor and turned right. Through the open door, he could see the others in the living room.

Felicity was looking out of the window, and Greg had turned his back to Julian, who was at the bar pouring another whiskey. As he dropped two cubes of ice into his glass, they sounded like they were splintering. His eyes locked on Earl's.

"Here it is," Samantha said.

She'd written Susy's number on a small piece of scented paper. The perfume was familiar.

"If there's anyone else you think of, friends, anyone

who may have known if Michael was in trouble, let me know."

"I will."

She followed him downstairs. As he opened the door, she said, "Find him."

Earl nodded and walked away from her and the brightly lit house.

CHAPTER 6

It was raining heavily the next day as Leonard Wells got off the 485 bus and walked to Kingston Hospital. Pools of water spilled out from the curbs, and a passing car splashed him as it sped through some lights. He tried to dry his trousers in the toilet, using paper towels that tore in his hands. Then he bought his mother some more flowers at the hospital shop. He took the lift to her floor, wondering why they'd called to say they were keeping her in longer.

He could see Pam Smythe through the glass doors before he got to the desk. She glimpsed Leonard, flushed, and picked up the phone. Leonard walked past her, determined to remain quiet, see his mother, and leave. She'd be out in the next day or so, he thought. The nurses and doctors all stuck together, like those army snobs who sent other men out to die. There was no point arguing with them. They did as they wished. England hadn't changed, England would never change, class divide ruled the nation.

Leonard approached his mother's bed. The curtains were drawn around it, and he waited, listening in case there was someone with her changing her bedpan. But it was silent, and he peeked through. Her bed was empty, and yesterday's flowers were wilting in a dry plastic vase.

He turned to see Dr. Truman standing a few feet away. Pam Smythe hovered behind him at the doorway.

"Where's my mother?"

"She's been moved to another ward," Truman said.

"Which one?"

"I'm afraid you're going to have to leave."

"This is ridiculous. I got a call from you to say she was being kept in another day."

"I don't know anything about that."

"What's the matter with her? She was due to be released today."

Truman turned and said something to Pam Smythe that Leonard couldn't hear.

"Where's my mother?" Leonard said, tapping Truman on the shoulder.

"There was a complication in the night."

"What sort of complication?"

"She got hypothermia."

"Hypothermia, how the hell did the happen?"

"The elderly are vulnerable to it."

The old woman who had tutted yesterday was listening. "They left her out in the corridor all night, that's how she got it," she said. "Dreadful. She came back in a shocking state. They moved her over there to be nearer the heating."

"Is this true?"

"She hasn't been eating," Truman said.

"I read about it all the time, you forget you got patients, some of them are old. You let my mother freeze while you shagged Pam over there."

"Right, that's enough," Truman said.

But Leonard was walking away. He didn't hear him say, "Where are they?" to Pam, nor see her shrug her shoulders and go out into the corridor where two security guards were entering the ward.

Leonard went to the bed at the end. The curtains were drawn and a young oriental nurse came out and walked past him. Inside, his mother was sleeping. She looked shrunken, diminished by the experience, and Leonard's anger whipped at him like a rattle snake.

He laid the flowers on the night table, put his hand on her, and felt her breathing. The security guards came up behind him as she opened her eyes.

"Get me out of here Len," she said.

"I'll look after you, Mum."

He turned and saw the two guards and beyond them

Dr. Truman and Pam Smythe standing by the door.

"I'm going to have to ask you to leave," one of the guards said.

"And why is that?"

"You're causing a disturbance."

"Do I look like I'm causing a disturbance?"

"That's what the doctor says."

"Well, the doctor talks shit, don't he?"

"Come on. We'll have to escort you out."

The man doing the talking was big, taller than Leonard, but out of shape. He had a shaved head and stubble, and his breath smelled of onions. Behind him, the other security guard stood with his arms folded. He was black, strong, and his eyes wandered across Leonard's face, as if he'd seen him somewhere before and was trying to work out where.

"All right, I don't want to make any trouble," Leonard said, holding up his hands.

He leaned over, kissed his mother on the forehead, and left the ward, followed by the two guards. Truman was outside talking to a nurse, ignoring the event as if it was of no significance.

"Goodbye, Doctor Mengele," Leonard said and winked at him then blew him a kiss.

Truman turned his back.

They walked him to the lift and got in with him. It was empty and the larger guard pressed for the basement.

"I was in the army you know," Leonard said.

"That right?" the guard said, filling the enclosed space with the stench of onions.

"Yeah, and you know what it taught me?"

"You're not in the army now."

Leonard slammed his elbow into the guard's face, shattering his nose. Then he turned and kicked the black guard so hard between his legs he lifted him off the floor. The guard dropped to his knees, strands of saliva hanging from his open mouth as he groaned. Leonard kicked him in the stomach then turned as his colleague pulled out his baton.

"You gonna try that on me, fucker?" Leonard said.

The guard swung it at him. Leonard dodged, sending the guard off balance. Then Leonard caught him with a roundhouse in the jaw, and he crashed to the floor as the lift doors opened.

"You're a fucking bunch of pussies," Leonard said and walked out.

A mother with a buggy was trying to enter the lift. She stopped and put her hand to her mouth. She turned to look after Leonard, but he was moving fast toward the exit.

It was still raining outside as he walked to the bus stop.

"I'm sick of taking orders," he said as he pounded the paving stones, oblivious of the police sirens in the distance.

CHAPTER 7

Dave Ruby was a neatly dressed man with a pale complexion, brown hair, and a small moustache, who smelled of rose water. Earl met him the next day at eight a.m. at his office in Holland Park. Ruby showed him into a bright room with comfortable chairs and pastel walls, on which hung calming, neutral paintings of landscapes and sunsets. A tissue box sat on a wooden table.

Ruby sat down and placed his hands on his legs as Earl took the chair opposite him. He could hear the rumble of London traffic beyond the clean window behind Ruby, but it seemed contained, almost soporific in its muted noise, an irrelevance to the secure atmosphere of the therapist's room.

"Thank you for seeing me," Earl said. "I don't want you to feel professionally compromised, but Michael has been kidnapped, and I believe he's in danger."

"That is extremely disturbing. Michael's been through a lot. He succeeded in finding the roots of his problems, which is not always the case."

"And what were those roots?"

Ruby paused. "I weighed up my professional obligations after I received your call. I don't usually talk about my clients, but this is an exceptional case, and what I tell you is in confidence."

"Understood."

"He came to me suffering from an acute phobia, arachnophobia to be exact. He was an insomniac, whose nightmares troubled his days, and who'd taken to drinking heavily. He couldn't function. His fear was crippling. I used to see him check the corners of the room here when he came in. He sat with his feet tucked up on the chair, the same one you're sitting in now, in case a spider crawled up his leg. He said he felt them crawling all over him at night. He had no understanding of why the images disturbed him or their meaning in his personal drama."

"You managed to discover what it meant?"

Ruby nodded and took a sip of water. "Please help yourself, if you're thirsty," he said, gesturing to the bottle and spare glass on the table that sat between them.

"Thank you."

"Michael had other dreams, dreams that lay behind

the ones in which he was being eaten by spiders. I helped him access them by making him keep a journal."

"What were the other dreams?"

"He felt threatened by an elusive figure in a mask, a woman. She became known in our sessions as the spider woman. He felt she was watching him. He said she came into his room at night and rubbed tiny hairs across his skin. He described the sensation as like battery acid being poured on his flesh. He believed she was consuming him. The female arachnid eating the male after intercourse. Michael was afraid of sex. He dated girls. It lasted a few weeks. He hated body hair on women and ended his last attempt at a relationship when he discovered his girl-friend didn't shave."

"Would that be Susy?"

"I believe that was her name."

"So who is she, the spider woman?"

"This is where it all gets a little complicated, and I am unsure how much to say. I came under immense pressure toward the end of my therapy with him. His father became extremely angry with me. I even received a tele-phone phone call from him. He almost refused to settle the last bill."

"Why was that?"

"I helped Michael discover the roots of his phobia."

"And that involved his father?"

"Right." Ruby paused, his fingers steepled, his eyes on the table. "How much danger is Michael in?"

"I think he's in grave danger. The kidnapper has him and a friend of his locked in glass cages in a windowless room."

"Strange. The looking-glass self?"

"I'm sorry?"

"It's a theory that a person's self grows out of other's perceptions of him. It seems the kidnapper has constructed a sort of Panopticon. Jeremy Bentham designed one for prisoners. The idea was that they could be observed at all times. It instilled acute paranoia through total surveillance."

"What do you make of the use of it as a prison for Michael?"

"I'm not an expert on kidnapping, but I think whoever has abducted him is experimenting with his identity."

"What was Julian Villa so angry about?"

"The exposure Michael's big breakthrough produced."

"Exposure of Julian?"

"Yes. Michael's fear came from something quite simple. When he was six years old, his father took him to a party. Michael was a friend of the hostess's daughter. He and the daughter fell asleep in her room as the grownups partied late into the night. They were disturbed by a noise and went in search of their parents. Michael walked in on a scene his brain could make no sense of. His father was having sex with the hostess."

"This is where his phobia stems from?" Earl said.

Ruby nodded. "But this was no ordinary sex. What Michael saw was his father wearing a bondage hood and the woman in a mask. Both were naked, and neither recognisable to him. The woman's back was to him as he entered the room. There was blood on her buttocks. His father was holding a whip. Michael remembers his eyes staring at him from behind the leather hood. In that instant, the figures entered the deep psyche.

"Michael remembers running from the room, thinking he'd walked in on two monsters. The woman ran after him. Michael hid in a laundry closet. She opened the door and took his arm. Michael lashed out, and his hand touched her pubic area. It disturbed him. He'd never seen his mother naked. She pulled him up. She was trying to say something to him. He was terrified and could smell something on her breath, probably alcohol. 'You mustn't tell anyone,' she said. 'You mustn't tell anyone, or you won't have a mummy and daddy, do you understand me? We're not doing anything wrong. You will be like us one day.' He kept looking away from her and became fixated by the hair between her legs, which was at his eye level."

"So it wasn't Michael's mother?"

"No. Once Michael remembered the event, he recalled that, the evening he was taken to the party, his mother had the flu. He remembers saying goodbye to her and worrying about her."

"What did Julian say when he called you?"

"He accused me of being a charlatan, profiting from

his son's problems and trying to wreck his marriage. His behavior confirmed my success. I hadn't been employed by him as a marriage therapist, but to help his son. Julian Villa's behavior exhibited all the classic signs of a guilty man who's been found out."

"So the arachnophobia is connected to Michael's fear of pubic hair?"

"It's more complicated than that, but you're right, up to a point. Something else happened that night. Michael fled from her, entering a room at the end of the corridor. In the room was a large glass cage full of tarantulas. Michael wet himself as he stood there looking at them."

"And he's imprisoned in a glass cage."

"I think his kidnapper knows what happened that night."

"Both Michael and Abby had phobias."

Ruby leaned forward. "Abby Sheen?"

"Yes."

"She was Michael's friend. They both witnessed the same events. It was her mother who Julian was whipping. Felicity Sheen is the spider woman."

"No wonder Julian Villa was furious when it all came out."

"I've never met Felicity Sheen, but she's an odd woman with some odd habits. She's a collector of things."

"What sort of things?"

"Abby followed Michael into the room. There were

snakes in another cage. I think Felicity and Julian used them in their sex sessions. You know about Abby's phobia?"

"Snakes, I'm speaking to her therapist this afternoon."

"From what Michael told me, Abby's therapy was also a success, the revelation must have impacted on the Sheens' marriage."

"What happened in the Villas' marriage when you unearthed this?"

"I'm not entirely sure. But once Michael remembered seeing the woman in the mask, he began talking to his parents about it. His father became extremely angry and tried to stop the therapy. But it was like a snowball rolling downhill. All the memories began to pour out of the burst dam. Michael and Abby talked and, between them, they worked the rest out."

"This has been really helpful," Earl said, standing up.

"Will you let me know when you find them?"

"Of course."

"Michael has a lot of problems, most of them caused by his father. Julian Villa has bullied Michael his entire life, telling him he's useless, making him feel he's worthless. That's why the phobia got its roots so deep into his psyche. Of course, Julian knew what his son had witnessed and was chipping him away, piece by piece. Any attempts by Michael's mother to bolster his self-esteem went only so far. I think she does love her son, but she's been undermined by her husband."

"You know he hired a hypnotherapist for Michael after he'd finished therapy with you?"

"I didn't know that."

"Julian claims that was the success."

"He paid him to repress the memories."

"That's my guess."

"That's extremely sad."

"He also paid for Abby to see the same man."

"How sick."

"There's a lot I'm not being told."

"Julian Villa is, in my opinion, a sociopath. When he rang me, he insinuated he could have me bumped off."

"What exactly did he say?"

"'Most people are expendable. If you have the money, you can make a few calls and have them removed. Just you remember who you're working for, Mr. Ruby.'"

"Do you have any idea why someone would kidnap Michael?"

"No. But what I find interesting is he has kidnapped him and Abby."

"And what are the cages for?

"They represent the inability to hide, the loss of all privacy."

CHAPTER 8

The police went to Kingston Hospital that day. The security guard who'd pulled the baton on Leonard had a broken nose and jaw, the other guard had severely swollen testicles and torn stomach muscles. The camera in the lift was discovered to be faulty, displaying only grainy images.

"We come across that all the time," Inspector Jeff Palmer said to PC Brad Thomson.

Palmer was a tall man whose face was filled with a lifetime of suspicion. Thomson was shorter and, in conversation, weighed everything up, which made him seem reserved.

Palmer spoke to both the guards and then to Dr. Truman and Pam Smythe, while Thomson listened.

"So the man who assaulted your guards was visiting his mother?" Palmer said.

"Yes, he'd been asked to leave the hospital because he was intimidating Pam," Truman said.

"What's his name?"

Truman looked at Pam. "Do you know his name?"

"No, I don't."

"Better speak to his mother," Palmer said.

Truman nodded toward the far end of the room. "She's by the window."

The side of the bed facing them had a curtain drawn across it. Palmer paused as he and Thomson got there then peered round. He walked past the curtain, followed by Thomson. The bed was empty.

"Has she been moved?" Palmer said to Dr. Truman.

ℰↁℰↁ

As Dr. Truman checked the hospital records, Mary Wells was being given breakfast by her son Harry. He laid the tray on the bed in front of her.

"Here you go, Ma, tuck in, build up you strength, not like that hospital food."

"Bangers and bacon, ain't I a lucky girl?"

Mary cut one of the Walls sausages and chewed on it, her gaze wandering from Harry, as he drew the curtains on the spare room in his Surrey home.

"So Len let the flat did he?" Harry said.

"He means well, son."

"Yeah, I suppose."

"What went on between you two yesterday?"

"He called me, said he was taking you out of hospital, and I asked him how he was going to look after you. I had to keep reminding him you'd run out of the money Dad left you, and your pension ain't enough. 'The flat's gone, Len,' I said. He said he'd packed everything up. He called me from the flat, said he'd gone back for some clothes and Dad's picture."

"I'm on the council list."

Harry sat on the edge of the bed as Mary sipped her PG Tips. "Ma, that'll be a wait. They take ages these days, giving them to anyone except the people who live in this country. I'll look after you."

"What about my things?"

"After I got you from the hospital, I picked up the boxes Len had packed up for you at the flat. He let me in and just stood there, didn't say a word."

"Why did you upset him?"

"I didn't upset him. You know what he's like."

"He had an argument with a doctor."

"I know. He told me all about that on the phone, and he was right. I'm glad he called me. Hypothermia, what are they playing at? Once I heard that, there was no stopping me, I got straight in the car."

"He says he's bought a big house, in Kew."

"He's talking rubbish, Ma."

"Is he?"

"He ain't got that kind of money."

"Where's he living then?"

"I don't know, but you're staying here."

"How does Mandy feel about that?"

"Mandy's fine. She's out most of the time these days."

"Well, I'm glad I'm out of the bleeding ward."

"Bet you are, Ma."

"Try not to argue with Len."

"It's the other way round. He called me stuck up— *me*, of all people. I'm a plumber but he can't see that I got my money sticking my hands down people's drains and toilets."

CHAPTER 9

Dr. Truman was informed by the night staff that Mary Wells's son had discharged her.

"Tall chap, well built? He's been thrown out of the hospital and assaulted two guards," Truman said.

The nurse described a large plump man with a red face.

"She must have two sons," Truman said.

He checked the contact details Harry left.

"Did you read what he wrote?" Truman said angrily, shoving the page at the nurse. "Mickey Mouse, One Buck House, and this mobile number's probably bogus." He showed it to Palmer. "I'm sorry to say one of our staff has let us down."

Palmer took the note and said nothing, leaving a dent in Truman's professional status.

"Hardly inspiring," Palmer said to Thomson as he drove back to the station.

He dialed the number Harry had left and got a confused woman with a German accent.

"Is Harry Wells here?" Palmer said.

"No, who is this?"

Palmer apologised, explained he was a police Inspector and had been given a wrong number, and hung up. He shook his head while Thomson raised his eyebrows.

Their attempts to establish the whereabouts of Mary Wells's sons didn't get them far. Thomson found out that she had two sons, one named Harold, the other Spencer. There were no addresses registered for either. Harry had put his house in his wife's name for tax reasons. In fact, he put everything in Mandy's name. He didn't even have a bank account, and stashed all his earnings in Mandy's. He traded under the name Handy Plumbers. Leonard's first name was Spencer, but he never used it, not after the army. He'd adopted his middle name some years before. People knew him as Len.

Palmer did find out that Mary Wells had been renting a flat in Kew. They drove there and saw the Let sign. Palmer peered through the filthy windows at the empty living room.

They drove round to the letting agents. A man in a shiny suit who smelt of tobacco and chewed on a hangnail sat at his desk and glanced nervously at them as they walked in.

"Do you know a Mrs. Wells?" Palmer said.

"Oh, yes, nice lady. We just rented out her old place, lovely flat, two minute walk to Kew Gardens."

"Did you ever meet her sons?"

"I spoke to one of them. He told me they were moving."

"Did you catch his name?"

"He always called himself Mr. Wells."

"Say where he was moving to?"

"Yes, I did write it down. Nice area, Number Two, The Avenue."

"Do you have a contact number for him?"

"Only the number at the flat."

Number Two, The Avenue, was occupied by a family of four.

A tanned woman in a yellow blouse opened the door. She adamantly told them they'd lived there for eight years, had no intention of selling it, and that she'd never heard of anyone by the name of Wells.

"This one's a dead end," Palmer said to Thomson as they got back in their car. "Still, I don't think Mary Wells's son will be causing any more trouble at the hospital."

"If their cameras had been working, we'd have something to go on, and people wonder why the police find it hard to catch criminals," Thomson said.

ↄↄↄↄ

As they drove away, Leonard was calling Harry.

"How's Mum?"

"She's fine, Len."

"I might come and see her in a few days."

"That'll be fine."

"Then she can move in with me."

"Where?"

"I told you, I got a new gaff, big place."

"And how did you afford that?"

"I been doing some jobs."

"Doing what?"

"What is this?"

"Len, if you're gonna take care of Ma, you gonna have to do it proper."

"I took care of her at the hospital."

"You call beating up a couple of guards taking care of her?"

"She had hypothermia."

"I know, you told me, that's why I went and got her. I know what them wards are like."

"Can I speak to her?"

"She's sleeping."

"You always got to do it, don't ya?"

"Do what?"

"Big yourself up."

"I ain't."

"You told me you was going to look after Mum, you didn't ask."

"Because it's obvious where she should be."

"You're as bad as the rest of them."

"What's that supposed to mean?"

"I seen your type in the army."

"Don't cause any more aggro, Len."

"What you going to do, grass me up?"

"No, that's why I signed my name Mickey Mouse when I checked Ma out. I don't need the Old Bill sniffing round my gaff, nor does Mandy."

"Yeah, well, they got what they deserved."

"We all know you're handy with your fists, Len."

"You should have seen the way they were treating her in there."

"She'll be all right now."

"I visited her every day, Harry, not you, and you ride in and take charge."

"It ain't like that."

"Na, you just brush me to one side, don't you?"

Leonard was shaking as he ended the call. He stared at the floor of his room then picked up some dumb bells. He did sixty curls, staring at the picture of his father that he'd taken from the flat. It was the only adornment on the wall. The room was bare, consisting of a bed, a chair, some weights, and two suitcases with broken buckles.

CHAPTER 10

At two p.m. that afternoon Earl Blake was sitting in Marion Wakefield's plush office in Richmond. She was a matronly looking woman with a generous bust and inquisitive eyes that took you in above half-rim glasses. Earl sat opposite her in a deep chair.

Abstract paintings hung from the wall, and the window looked out at a well-maintained garden.

"How long was Abby in therapy with you?" Earl said.

"Two years."

"I understand she had a phobia of snakes."

"Ophidiophobia, yes. You said on the phone she's been kidnapped."

"Together with Michael Villa, whose name may be familiar to you."

"It is."

"I've spoken to Michael's therapist, Dave Ruby, and learned quite a lot about the background to his phobia."

"It's most interesting they've both been kidnapped."

"Michael and Abby both witnessed the same event," Earl said.

"They did, from what I can gather of Abby's account."

"Michael saw his father engaged in what sounds like sadomasochistic sex with Abby's mother. According to his therapist, his arachnophobia stems from the event."

"Children who witness adult activities of this nature often develop phobic reactions. The mind locks in on an image it can't define."

"I think the kidnapper knows what happened to them, that's why it's important I understand what they saw that night. In your opinion what caused Abby's ophidiophobia?"

"Seeing Julian Villa's erect penis followed by the cage full of snakes. She describes waking up and going to look for her mother with Michael. She went into her parent's bedroom first, Michael was behind her. She saw a man touching a naked woman who was wearing a mask. The man had a hood on and he frightened Abby. She says she saw something squirt from his penis. I suspect Felicity Sheen was masturbating Julian Villa as the children walked in on them, and he ejaculated."

"Did she describe running after Michael into another room?"

"Yes, full of spiders and snakes."

"What do you know of Abby's relationship with her mother? Apparently, Michael went through years of bullying by his father."

"Abby's mother didn't bully her. Abby developed low self-worth because she was always comparing herself to her mother, who is extremely beautiful. Abby felt she couldn't live up to her. Her father is a hard-working man who sadly compounded the problem by saying how beautiful his wife was. Abby is far from unattractive. She just doesn't think she is. She developed a fear of sex. The therapy helped, and she had a boyfriend when my sessions with her ended. But I think she hates sex and has used men simply for her self-esteem."

"Did you know Julian Villa threatened Dave Ruby?"

"No, threatened how?"

"He was furious when his affair with Felicity Sheen came out. He hinted he would have him hurt, and then he paid for them to see a hypnotherapist."

"Them?"

"Yes, he sent both Michael and Abby to see someone who, I believe, was paid to erase the memories."

"How sinister."

"Do you know how Felicity reacted when Abby remembered what had caused her fear of snakes?"

"She was, from what I can gather, devastated, and spent hours alone in her room crying. This made Abby feel guilty. Her father, Greg, became silent, withdrawn, and threw himself into work. Abby said she heard him arguing with Julian Villa on the phone one evening. She also said she heard him tell Felicity he forgave her."

"Can you think of a possible reason someone would kidnap both of them?"

"No."

"They're being held in two glass cages."

"Glass, did you say?"

"Yes, the Villas and the Sheens received a film of them in a bare room, locked in glass enclosures of some sort."

"What is the ransom?"

"Four million."

"Has this been taken to the police?"

"The parents are nervous the kidnapper will harm Michael and Abby if they do that."

"Something strange happened a few weeks ago. It's the only thing I can think of that might link the kidnapping to the therapy Abby underwent with me. My office was burgled. The thief took various files containing case notes on my patients, among them Abby's."

"How many were taken?"

"Four, but the others were all old files, years old. Abby's was the only recent one. That was all that was stolen. My computer was here, and some of these paintings are valuable."

"And presumably these notes would have contained information about what Abby saw?"

"Detailed notes about the event."

"Mentioning what Julian Villa and Felicity Sheen were doing that night?"

"Yes, as seen through Abby's eyes."

"Then someone has a particular interest in obtaining that information," Earl said.

"Julian Villa seems a likely candidate."

"I agree, except I would have thought he'd want Michael's notes not Abby's."

"Michael's therapist wasn't burgled?"

"He didn't mention it."

"Then someone wanted to know exactly what Abby saw."

"Or they wanted to find out how to mess with her mind."

CHAPTER 11

Leonard Wells visited his mother that afternoon. Harry let him in and they stood awkwardly in the hallway, waiting for each other to speak, then Leonard went upstairs. He spent a few hours talking to his mother, making sure she was all right. It was early evening when he left. Harry was watering his roses in the front garden, and Leonard paused beneath a pink sky as his brother turned off the water and set the hose down on the gravel drive.

"So, Len, staying for some supper?" Harry said, wiping his hands on the back of his jeans.

"Na, I'll think I'll head back."

"Back where?"

"To my gaff, Harry."

"You know, it don't have to be like this."

"Like what?"

"Between us."

"You like to think you know best, don't you?"

"You can see she's okay. She ain't got no hypothermia now, she gets decent food, she's in a warm room. Don't that make you happy?"

"Suppose."

"Come on, Mandy'll be back in an hour. She always liked you."

"I ain't hungry."

"What's happened to you, Len?"

"Harry, I wanted to look after Mum."

"She's better off here."

"You always want to make me feel like I ain't no good."

"No, I don't."

"You done all right for yourself, but you'll see."

"Look, I know what happened to your mate in the army messed up your head."

"You don't know the half of it. He was screaming for help. He shattered one of my ear drums. They sent us the wrong way. I had a plastic bag over his guts, trying to keep them in. They all lied, they all covered their own backs. The men who send us off to die ain't soldiers. It's the same story I see with the doctors. They do what they want and get away with it."

Leonard's eyes were glowing and had a reddish cast

as Harry looked at him. He could see the sun setting in his brother's pupils.

Just then a black Mercedes pulled up, shredding the gravel. A blonde woman in a tight-fitting blue jacket and skirt got out. The shape of her buttocks was outlined by the cut of her skirt as she bent and reached in for her handbag. She wore too much makeup and had large silver earrings dangling from her ears. She raised her sunglasses, placed them on top of her head, then walked toward Leonard in high heels.

"Hello, Len," Mandy said. "Coming in for a drink?"

"Na, I better get off."

She placed her palm on his chest. "Come on, Len, it'll be like the old days."

"They're gone, Mandy, and they ain't coming back."

ↄↄↄↄ

Earl called Dave Ruby and asked if he'd had a break-in. When Ruby said no, Earl explained what had happened at Marian Wakefield's office.

That evening, Earl met Susy at the Mango Lounge in Earls Court. He found her, as she said he would, near the bar surrounded by friends.

"I'll grab my vodka and we can go and talk over there," she said, pointing to a small table near the door.

Susy was a petite and extremely pretty brunette in her twenties, who wore a faded denim jacket and a red mini-skirt. Her eyes were glazed, and she was drunk. She swayed as she walked away from her friends. The pub was noisy, and Earl had to strain to hear what she was saying.

"You said Michael's been kidnapped," she said, fingering an ice cube in her glass with a bright pink varnished fingernail.

"He has."

"That's awful. He's a really nice bloke. I liked him."

"Did he say anything to you about anyone following him?"

"No."

"Is there anyone you can think of who might want to harm him?"

She shook her head and sipped from her glass. "No. Then I only went out with him for a few weeks. I was really upset when he broke it off."

"What happened?"

"Between us? I don't know. He was funny, shy, you know. I thought he was seeing someone else. He called me one day and said he didn't want to go out with me anymore."

"When was the last time you saw him?"

"About a month go."

"Did you ever meet his parents?"

"Once. The mum was really nice."

"And his father?"

"I don't know. I felt his eyes all over me, you know."

"Do you know Abby Sheen?"

"He mentioned her to me. I never met her."

"She's been kidnapped with Michael."

"This is about money, right?"

"I think it's more complicated than that."

"He will be all right?"

"I hope so."

"But you don't know where he is?"

"I don't."

"And this is what you do? You're a private investigator."

"That's right."

Earl could see a young man with dark hair standing at the bar, staring at them. Susy glanced over at him.

"I should have met you somewhere quieter, shouldn't I? I didn't know who you were, you know? You get pranksters."

"You did the right thing."

"Let me know when you find Michael, okay?"

"Of course, thank you for meeting me. If you think of anything, call me."

Earl handed her his card.

"I will," Susy said, slipping it in her breast pocket.

e⁄ɔe⁄ɔ

Earl had called Miguel earlier that day. Miguel said he could meet him for a few minutes at Richmond University. Earl rode the Ninja there from Earls Court, dodging the traffic, weaving in and out of cars, and tearing away from amber lights. Miguel had said he would be in the coffee shop.

He was a dark-haired man in his late twenties with sharp features. And what he had to say didn't take long.

"You say Abby has been abducted?"

"She has."

"Look, I only went out with her for a few weeks. That's how she was. She ditched guys when they got too close."

"Did Abby ever say anything to you that could shed light on why she's been kidnapped?"

Miguel swirled the coffee in his cup. "Said? No Abby didn't say anything."

"You didn't part on good terms."

"We didn't part on any terms. That bitch has got hang ups."

"What sort of hang ups?"

"I don't know, maybe she's a lesbian."

"You can't think of anyone who may want to harm her?"

"I don't know. Maybe some guy she messed around."

"When was the last time you saw her?"

"Two weeks ago, when she said she wanted to be single. Then I saw her kissing some guy at the bar here."

"Can you describe him?"

"He was dark complexioned. I couldn't see his face."

"Was he tall, what age was he?"

"Like I say, he could have been anyone. She had her tongue down his mouth, poor sucker."

"Did you ever meet Michael Villa?"

"Her friend? No, she talked about him all the time, said he got her when no one else did. It's like they shared some secret."

"What do you think Abby was hiding?"

"It was sexual, you know? I've slept around and you know which ones like it. She didn't like it. She used to keep her eyes closed."

"Did you ever meet her parents?"

"I met the mother. Now, I could tell she liked it, good-looking woman. The father came in as I was leaving, said hello, that was it, I think Abby has a complex around her mother."

"Why do you say that?"

"She's better looking than Abby, that's why Abby plays with guys, maybe that's why she's been kidnapped."

"Who do you think has kidnapped her?"

"Who knows? I think she messed with some guy's head, and he's teaching her a lesson."

"Do you think Abby needs to be taught a lesson?"

"Look, I ain't done it."

"I'm not saying you have."

"I gotta go. We finished?"

"She's been kidnapped with Michael."

"No shit?"

"If you see the guy you saw kissing her again, can you ask him to call me?"

"It'll be the first thing on my agenda."

"I understand how you feel about Abby, but she is in danger. Please call me if you think of anything," Earl said, rising and placing his card on the table.

Miguel shrugged. "Sure, but I won't."

CHAPTER 12

Leonard unpacked his suitcases in his room. He opened the first one and removed the stack of *Soldier* magazines, placing them in neat piles on the floor. Many of them were tattered and yellowing. A soldier in camouflage stared at him from the front cover of the issue that sat on top of the pile.

The second case contained his clothes and army uniforms, which he removed and held up, then hung in the cheap cupboard he'd bought that morning. Outside, it began to rain. Leonard lifted his dumbbells from the floor and began his curls. His eyes weren't focused on the room at all, but the battle he'd fought in. He wasn't looking at the bar or the concrete floor but the men he'd killed and his mate Kenny lying on the ground screaming, his face contorted and unrecognisable. Len curled the bells, sweat gathering on his toned back, his shoulders as hard as rocks, his forearms corded with veins.

He set the weights down and lifted the barbell he'd bought that morning. He'd taken a plank of wood from a timber yard and laid it across the room, one end on the edge of the bed, the other on a chair. Now he lay down on it and pressed two hundred pounds. When he finished, he showered in the small cubicle at the rear of the room, then he put on a pair of Levis and a blue T-shirt. Sitting on his bed, he ate a cheese sandwich he'd bought at the local petrol station, then he went out and took the bus to Kingston.

తింఒ

Earl met Stuart Parkes that afternoon. Parkes had an office in Kensington, a room with no paintings on the wall that was decorated in a light pastel blue.

He was a slightly overweight man who wore a dress shirt and dark trousers with a neat crease across the front. He smiled as he greeted Earl and led him through the reception area where a pretty woman was typing rapidly, her eyes fixed on her computer screen. Parkes leant against his desk. The rain pelted the window like small stones.

"How can I help, Mr. Blake?" he said.

"I believe you saw Michael Villa and Abby Sheen some weeks ago."

"I did."

"I've been hired by their parents, as I mentioned."

"They've been kidnapped, you said. Nasty business. Who would do such a thing?"

"That's what I'm trying to find out."

Parkes leafed through a large hardback book on his desk. "Well, the last time I saw Michael was two weeks ago, today, at two o'clock. I saw Abby that afternoon at four."

"Were you aware they'd been in therapy for two years prior to seeing you?"

"Yes, of course. Julian Villa asked me to help. He believed they'd had memories implanted in them and were highly disturbed by what he called a fantasy event."

"What is your view?"

"About what?"

"The reality of what they thought they remembered."

"It's hard to say. Therapists do sometimes go with a popular theory, and patients can be suggestible."

"Do you think a therapist can induce a memory of something that didn't take place?"

"Yes, it has happened."

"What about their phobias?"

"I help people by allowing them to forget, that's what I did."

"Their therapists say they were disturbed because they couldn't remember what had happened, that their minds had focused on a phobic reaction that was a distortion of an event they had no point of reference for. Is it possible that, by repressing their memories, you've reverted them to the condition they were in before they sought help?"

"Mr. Blake, the mind represses things because it needs to."

"So you believe they shouldn't have remembered what happened?"

"If it happened, yes."

"And what if it didn't?"

"Then I've removed something that has no reality at all. The mind is fragile, memories are unreliable. I try to steer patients away from things that are troubling them, and that sometimes includes removing desires and what they believe are memories. Sometimes I also try to help people remember."

"But in Michael and Abby's case you were hired to make them forget."

"I hope you find them."

"Do you have any idea why someone would kidnap them?"

"No, I don't."

"I believe their kidnapper knows about their mental history."

"Why do you say that?"

"Abby's therapist's office was burgled a few weeks ago, Abby's case notes were stolen."

"Presumably this kidnapper wants to be paid."

"Yes, but I also think he plans to torture them."

"Torture them?"

"The parents were sent a film of them. They're being held in glass cages."

"It seems an unusual approach."

"It is."

CHAPTER 13

Felicity Sheen was drunk when the phone rang at seven p.m. She was wearing an old cream-colored blouse, on which the cotton had thinned so that it was almost sheer, and a pair of tight-fitting jeans. Her hair hung loose over her shoulders. She sipped from her glass of Pinot Grigio as she picked up the phone.

"Hello?"

"It's Samantha."

"Any news?"

"Earl's spoken to the therapists. He didn't say much, except he believes the kidnapping is connected."

"Connected how?"

"He didn't say. Is Greg there?"

"I know you prefer to talk to him, but we've been friends for years.

"Is that why you fucked my husband?"

"Samantha, please."

Felicity's words were slurred as Greg approached and snatched the receiver out of her hand.

"I'll speak to her."

"Fine, I'm only Abby's mother."

"Hello, Samantha?" Greg said, turning his back on Felicity.

"Earl's talked to the therapists."

"Well, I think it's about time we pay this man and get our children back."

CHAPTER 14

Abby had her hands pressed to the glass as she talked to Michael, who was standing at the front of his cage. There were vents in the front of each cage, allowing them to talk.

"How long have we been here?" Abby said.

"I'm not sure. He took my watch."

"Mine too."

"I think it's a couple of days."

"I remember what happened, or some of it."

"Do you remember getting here?"

"No."

"What is this room?"

"It must be the basement of a house."

"I remember the strange man who stopped us," Michael said.

"Yes, he said something about his cat being run over,

and you went to look in the back of his van, then it all went black."

"You know how I love cats. His van was open and I climbed inside. There was a shape at the end but when I got to it I saw it was just a piece of fur. Then I heard him getting in. He was carrying you and dumped you on the ground. He came over to me and put something over my mouth."

"What does he want?"

"I don't know."

"He must have planned this," Abby said. "Think how long it must have taken to make these cages."

"It's plexiglass," Michael said, tapping the inside. "He's secured it to the ground with brackets and bolts. I've tried budging it but it's impossible. I reckon it's shatter proof."

"It gives me the creeps, the way he built in the loos at the back."

"Who would want us kidnapped?"

"I'm scared he's going to touch me."

"We've got to believe we'll get out of here, Abby."

"If only we could find out what he wants, but he hasn't spoken to us."

"The roof's opening, he's coming down."

CHAPTER 15

The second film arrived two days later. Earl went to Kensington at eight p.m. Samantha looked pale as she opened the door and, for a brief moment, he wanted to reach out and take her in his arms. He knew that vulnerable look from long ago. Upstairs in the living room, the curtains were drawn. Greg sat on a chair at the far end of the room, his legs crossed, his back straight. Julian was at the bar. Felicity swayed across the room, holding a Martini, her delicate fingers wrapped around the fragile stem of the glass. They each seemed to be separating in their grief.

"Good to see you," Felicity said, planting a wet kiss on Earl's cheek.

He caught Samantha's angry glare.

"Drink, Earl?" Julian said.

"I'll have a beer."

Julian poured Earl a Heineken and brought it over to him. "The kidnapper's upped his game," he said.

"It's horrible," Samantha said.

Greg got up and walked over to them. "Why don't we show him the film? I want to pay this bastard."

"I'd like to do a lot more than that," Julian said.

They went into the room next door. Julian picked up the remote control and pressed play.

The first image was of Abby, looking terrified. It was just her face.

"Daddy, Mummy, I'm okay, but he says he's going to do things to me, things I have nightmares about. Pay him, please pay him, do exactly as he asks, and I will be okay."

The film flickered then showed Michael. Again just his face.

"Hi, Mum and Dad. He hasn't done anything, but he knows how to hurt us, mentally. He told me what he's going to do if he doesn't get the money. Don't mess him around."

The camera swung away from him, around the four bare walls. It showed a man in a leather hood. He stared at the camera with expressionless eyes. Then the film stopped.

Earl noticed Julian's hands shaking as he turned it off.

"He's going to torture them," Felicity said.

"They said he hasn't hurt them," Samantha said.

Greg put his glass down. "We pay him now."

"Have you received instructions of how?" Earl said.

"Yes, and we did as he asked."

"What does he want you to do?"

"Greg and I received a text today at the same time, six o'clock," Julian said. "I've kept the number it was sent from, but I suspect it won't lead anywhere. He probably bought a phone with cash and threw it away afterward. The text said the same thing to both of us. It gave an email address phobiafun@gmail.com and a password, spidersandsnakes. It told us to log in and go to drafts, read the instructions, then delete the message when we'd both read it."

"What did the message say?" Earl said.

"Drop the four million off in non-sequential notes in the bin behind the warehouse in Royal Park. It gave an address. I've checked it. It's part of an industrial area. Greg is to go there, drop it at midnight tomorrow, and walk away. No police. He said if Greg brings anyone, he will kill Abby and Michael after he makes them suffer."

"Can you get the money by then?"

"I can," Greg said.

"I need longer," Julian said.

"How long?"

"Two days."

"What did you do with the email?" Earl said.

"I deleted it," Julian said. "Once I'd spoken to Greg and checked that he'd read it. I didn't want to risk making this man angry."

Earl nodded. "It's a way of sending a message without it going over the net. The secret services use it. The kidnapper is being extremely careful not to get traced."

"Do you think if we pay him, he'll let them go?" Julian said.

"He might."

"I need more time."

"What do you mean, you need more time?" Greg said. "Our children's lives are at risk."

"The money's tied up. I can't just access it at such short notice."

Greg walked over to the bar and poured himself a gin and tonic.

"Take two million, leave a message saying the rest will follow," Earl said.

"Then what?"

"I'll follow Greg, and tail the kidnapper. If I can get a registration number from his vehicle, then we can use it to trace him."

"What if he sees you?"

"Then I'll take him on."

CHAPTER 18

The following day, Earl managed to get a fix on the location of the mobile phone the text was sent from. He pulled it out of a dustbin in Royal Park. He wore gloves, took it away, and checked it for prints but it was clean. It was also unregistered.

He met the Villas and Sheens at six p.m. in Kensington. Each time he went there the tension mounted. They strained to hide their hostilities, but their bodies were taut and their eyes evasive.

"You said you found the phone," Julian said.

"The kidnapper wiped it down."

"Do you think he's holding Michael and Abby in Royal Park?"

"It's possible. It's a good area for the drop-off, that

part of Royal Park has a lot of disused industrial buildings."

"I'll get the money together," Greg said.

"I checked the email address he sent the instructions
from," Earl said. "Either he's changed the password or
deleted the account."

Felicity was pouring herself another glass of wine at
the bar. She came over to him and stood inches from his
face, her eyes hazed. "What if I can't get my daughter
back?"

"You will."

"Do you think he's punishing us?"

"That's not how kidnappers think."

"That's how it feels, for my sins, my daughter is
locked in a cage."

"How could he be punishing you?" Julian said, putting his glass down hard on a glass topped table.

Felicity went outside, followed by Samantha. Earl
followed them, wanting to get away from the argument
he felt was about to explode, wanting to gather his
thoughts. He found Samantha in the hallway.

"We're a sick bunch, aren't we?" she said. "You
must be relieved you didn't get hitched to me after all."

He said nothing, just went downstairs and out into
the cool night that smelled of roses shedding perfume and
of freshly cut grass.

He could make out Felicity at the end of the front
garden. She came over to him, placed one hand on his

arm, and sipped from her glass. Her skin looked like alabaster and her mouth was full and rich like a strawberry that had been cut in half. Her eyes were half way between despair and decadence, as if the latter helped ease the pain.

"You know, I am the sort of woman who needs to be told what to do."

"I'm doing everything I can to find Abby."

"I have desires some men find appealing, some men find unaccountable. I'm not an account, I keep telling myself, a good lay perhaps, but I'm not a series of numbers. Greg used to be an accountant, before he became an architect. He likes maths, he does the maths on me in bed once in a while. He counts the steps to my distant heart. He tries to arouse me with a numeric rhythm, but it doesn't work. He doesn't understand my architecture, my inner space. Funny. The architect. He builds things. That's how he and Julian make so much bloody money. Greg is a good designer of space. He's never been inside me, not really. Does my idle talk shock you?"

"No, is it meant to?"

"It's all true, you know, the kinky sex scenes. I do things, I do them to reach myself, to touch myself inside. Does it turn you on, Earl? Evasive Earl, I wonder what your habits are. No doubt you've heard about me. I have a reputation among these friends of mine, who hate my guts."

"I think Samantha and Greg feel betrayed."

"They do. They wear it well, don't you think?"

"And you? Do you feel guilty?"

"I do. I need something to take it away. Will you help me?"

"Most kidnappers make a mistake."

"Oh, I know about mistakes. Do you enjoy looking inside people's lives? Are they facts to you? Or stories you take way and chew on?"

"Neither."

"Yes, Julian was with me that night. He wants people to believe it never happened, but Greg knows it did, and so does Samantha. She's angry, she wants an affair. I think she has her eye on you, Earl. Imagine how Julian would feel about that. He gets angry. I know him. I had my hand on his cock that night. He was coming as Abby walked in and saw the snake."

"I think it's time for me to go."

"What a whore her mother is. I enjoy the sex, you see? It takes me away from myself long enough for me to forget."

"Forget what?"

"Who I really am."

"And what is that?"

"At least Abby can console herself with knowing she's my moral superior. She's compared herself to me, my looks, I used to be a model, you know."

"You think that's how Abby sees you?"

"He'd been whipping me until my buttocks bled. It turns him on, you know."

"You enjoy being punished?"

"I do, Earl, I do, but I don't want this, not my daughter in a cage."

"I'm going to take the money to him and track him."

"I need to hurt myself to stop this. I can't bear it. Are you the sort of man?" She came closer to him and put her index finger under his chin. The tops of her breasts looked damp in the moonlight, and her dress rose and fell with her breathing. "Let me see. I don't think you are that kind of man, Earl. When it all came out, Samantha screamed at me. Greg made it harder, in a way. He was so nice. He loves me. He can't bear the idea of not having me, so he's tried to accept it. We're both greedy women who made disastrous marriage choices."

"You both married for money?"

"Greg wasn't wealthy when I met him, Julian's influence led to that. No, Greg was the most down-to-earth uncorrupted man I'd ever met. I was lying to myself, you see. I'd given up drugs, we all used them to stay slim. Do I look fat to you? I don't need drugs, my addictions are of a more carnal nature. I thought I'd become someone else if I married a certain type of man. Instead, I've ruined him. There's something so reassuring about his decency. He is a decent man. It makes me sick, makes me loathe myself as the slut that I am."

Samantha opened the door and stood there, haloed by the bright lights behind her. Felicity turned and walked toward her, blotting out Samantha's image.

CHAPTER 17

Leonard followed them from the hospital at eight p.m. It was his second stakeout, and he was standing under an awning, looking at the moon crawl behind some rain clouds when he saw them leave in a group. Pam Smythe was talking to a black female nurse and Doctor Truman to a small colleague, who walked ahead of him, nodding, his hands in his pockets. Leonard tailed them to the Willoughby Arms. Before he'd attacked the guards, he heard one of the nurses talking about a get-together that week. It looked like this was the night the doctors mixed with the nurses.

The pub was packed. Doctor Truman went over to talk to some colleagues who were at the bar sipping pints. Leonard went to the far side of the bar, ordered a coke, and sat at a table at the back, keeping Pam and Truman in view. The evening crawled by like a poisonous snake, as Leonard sat among the company he most detested, the privileged who used and disposed of others. He watched their mannerisms, their conceits, and he saw things that soothed his mind, entering a private word where he had his own cinema on which he played his secret films. He watched Pam flirt briefly with Truman, adjusting his tie.

They left in separate groups. Leonard tailed Pam to the bus stop. He sat behind her and watched her play with her mobile phone all the way to Mitcham. He followed her a few blocks to a street filled with skips piled with bricks. He watched her enter a house, and the lights coming on.

He jotted down the address on the back of the receipt for the weights he'd bought, writing the street name and number neatly with a biro he'd taken from a betting shop. Then he inspected the walkway that ran along the side of house and the ease of access to the rear garden.

He took the bus back, returned to his room, and sat among his magazines. A copy of *The Sun* lay open on the bed, its pages crumpled from when he'd thrown it at the wall.

An article about the NHS began, "Nurses are complaining about the way they are treated." It went on to detail situations in which nursing staff felt their authority was being undermined by the families of patients who were unhappy about their care. In one ward, an elderly woman was left unattended for a day. When her relatives complained, the nurse said they were rude and threating. The relatives said she had no idea about human dignity...

CHAPTER 18

Earl followed Greg to Royal Park, hanging back a few cars. Greg parked his Audi a few minutes' walk from the spot where he was to drop off the money. Earl pulled the Ninja to the side of the road and watched Greg walk ahead of him. Earl looked up at the rooftop of a disused factory, scanning the windows of nearby buildings. The street was deserted, and nothing stirred, except the litter that floated spectrally away from the gutter, crawling along the stained pavement, scraping the concrete. Earl rode on, past the warehouse.

It was eleven p.m. when Greg entered the enclosed area between two warehouses and set the bag on the ground. Earl had checked the site the day before and found there was another way into the area. He parked the

Ninja half a mile away and proceeded to climb up a drainpipe onto a roof. Then he ran across four warehouses and climbed down a fire escape ladder to where Greg was waiting.

Earl took up his position at the mouth of an alley at the far end, some hundred feet away from where the money would be left. He watched Greg open the bin and place the large bag inside. Then Greg left, and Earl heard the engine of the Audi start up and fade. He waited until midnight.

Earl saw no movement at all, merely the scudding clouds and a rat crossing the concrete ground that lay between him and the bin holding the two million pounds in cash. He'd brought a blackjack with him, a foot long piece of lead covered in electrician's tape with a rubber handle.

It was almost one a.m. when a figure entered the area. He came in from the other side, walked quickly toward the bin, and opened it. He was tall and wore a dark coat with a hood low over his face, jeans, trainers, and black leather gloves. He lifted the bag out and left.

Earl edged out of the alley and raced after him. As he got to the end of the warehouse, he saw the man's back disappearing at a bend. Earl pursued, gaining speed. He ran for about half a mile, following the man through a series of alleys and turns that dissected the industrial area and brought them out into a street.

As Earl left the alley, a fist smashed him in the side

of the head. The next thing he knew, he was staring at a sullen moon and the side of his face was wet.

CHAPTER 19

Abbey was asleep when the man in the leather hood entered the room from the ceiling. She stared at Michael who lay on his side, his face pressed to the glass wall of his cage. As the man walked toward her, she retreated to the back of her cage. He was wearing black leather gloves and he held up a box covered in a black cloth.

Then he knocked on Michael's cage. Michael jumped up and looked around. The kidnapper had his back to Abby as he lifted the cover off the box. Michael began to scream. Abby couldn't see what the kidnapper was holding until he turned round and walked toward her. Then she saw the glass box full of tarantulas.

He gripped the metal handle at the top in one hand

and held a mobile phone in the other. His concealed eyes measured her reaction, and she began to feel like an insect in an experiment. He put the box down in front of her and then he inserted a key in the roof of her cage. She hadn't seen the lock since it was obscured by the wooden structure surrounding the toilet at the back. It opened a large panel of glass.

He opened the lid of the box and tipped the tarantulas into Abby's cage. He began filming it on his mobile phone. The tarantulas fell on top of each other, crawling across one another's backs, their bellies bloated as they scuttled across the glass floor. Abby inched away and pressed her back against the front of her cage.

"I know you're not afraid of spiders. It's snakes that make you terrified, Abby," the kidnapper said, his voice metallic, and devoid of intonation.

She turned round and tried to see into his eyes. "You said you'd only do this if you weren't paid."

"I haven't been paid."

"What do you want from us?"

"I want you to know what it feels like to be made of glass."

"I know what it feels like. I don't believe my father hasn't paid you."

"It's your father, Michael, who's let you down. No, don't stare at the ground. I want you to watch Abby."

Michael was shaking as he forced himself to glance in the direction of Abby but the tarantulas were everywhere and he looked away.

"Look at her, or I'll hurt her. Or are you willing to let that happen?"

Michael raised his head and looked at them. One had begun to crawl up her leg. She screamed and flicked it off with her right shoe. Then she went to the back of her cage and got some toilet roll. Another tarantula got onto her trainer and she scraped it off with the roll.

"If I'm not paid soon," the kidnapper said to Michael, "I'll put them in your cage."

"My father must have paid you, he's a wealthy man."

"Maybe he doesn't like you. Maybe he wants you here with me and all the creepy crawlies that make you piss your bed."

Abby began to scream. The tarantulas were crawling on her legs and her efforts to repel them were becoming wilder.

"You're in the glass house now," the kidnapper said. "All you see is yourself, your fear, the thing that held you together. They paid, didn't they? They paid for a cure. I've brought you here to put back those pieces of you that make you who you are, phobias and all. I'm taking the cure away."

"You can kill people with fear," Michael said, "without even laying a hand on them."

"I know, keep watching."

The kidnapper stopped filming and climbed up the ladder that rose into the ceiling and the darkness beyond it. He stepped onto the roof of Abby's cage and then jumped inside it, squashing two tarantulas beneath his boots. He removed a can of deodorant from his coat pocket and a Zippo lighter. He pressed the button on the can and flicked the Zippo alight, then he set the flame against the spray. He burned the tarantulas alive.

He removed them from Abby's legs with his gloved hands and aimed the flame at them. They dropped to the floor and shriveled into scorched balls that looked like sultanas. He burned them off the walls, and out of the corners of the cage, leaving burn marks on the glass. Michael retched into his cage, spraying the glass floor.

"Imagine them on your naked body," the kidnapper said to Abby. "Next stop, it's snakes." He pressed the can again, releasing two hissing squirts of deodorant into the air.

Abby thought she was gazing at a jackal in a leather hood, who was masquerading as the man who filled her sleep with snakes. As he locked the top of her cage and ascended into the ceiling, the glass house assumed the intensity of a dream to Abby and Michael. It was peopled with chimeras and hidden fears. And they longed for a window onto the world outside, a window made of glass they could smash.

CHAPTER 20

Earl wasn't badly hurt. The punch had broken the skin on his temple but there was no need for stitches.

He met them the next day in Richmond at two p.m. Greg had an urgent meeting and said he was unable to travel into Kensington. Felicity opened the door in a blue chiffon dress and matching shoes and stood there staring at his face.

"They're all upstairs, the usual company. Did he hurt you?" she said.

"It's a bruise, that's all."

"They can be hard to get rid of," she said, wagging a finger at him, then walked upstairs swaying her hips.

Earl followed her into the living room, which was

packed with antiques and family pictures. He sat down on the sofa next to a table covered with photographs, and noticed one had been turned to face the wall. Greg was standing with his arms folded across his chest, Julian was sitting in a chair, checking his mobile phone. Samantha was standing next to him and walked over to Earl.

She looked agitated and spilled some wine as she bent to whisper in his ear. "Julian and Greg gave been fighting, I hate coming here where it all happened."

Her lips brushed his face, then she touched his bruise and let her eyes linger on his. She smelled of honey and pine needles, her mouth was open and moist, and she was breathing as if aroused. Felicity was pouring herself another glass of wine, watching Samantha. Greg tried to say something to her, but she turned away as Julian got up abruptly from his chair and walked across the room.

"So you lost him," he said.

"He was a fast runner. He made me out and jumped me. He knew the area," Earl said.

"So what happens to our kids now?"

"He'll make contact."

"What if he kills them?"

"He won't if you come up with the money," Greg said. "Earl, can I get you a drink?"

"Thanks, I'll have a beer."

Greg opened a can of Pilsner, poured it into a glass, and handed it to Earl. "How much longer is it going to take you, Julian? I've done my bit," he said.

"I'm working on it."

"Yes, you boys have both done your bit," Felicity said.

"What's that supposed to mean?"

"Look, Julian, why don't you stop squabbling?" Samantha said.

"I'm not the one who started it."

"It depends what you're referring to," Greg said.

"Our sociable veneer is cracking. You two can hardly stand to be in the same room together," Felicity said.

"Well we're not as chummy as you and Samantha."

Earl stood up. "This isn't going to get Michael and Abby back."

"No, you're quite right," Julian said.

"He's got half the money, he'll want the rest."

"I can get it in a few days. I assume he'll wait."

"He's got the note Greg put in the bag."

"Once he's paid, how do we know if we'll ever see Michael and Abby again?"

"When we arrange to send the remaining money we ask, for a handover. If he doesn't exchange Michael and Abby, he doesn't get the money."

As Earl sipped his beer, he peered at the picture with its back to him. On the other side was Greg, his arm around Felicity, both of them smiling beneath the glass.

CHAPTER 21

The next film arrived a day later. They watched as the camera panned onto Abby and the tarantulas, and Earl listened to the gasps of both mothers.

"This creep knows about their therapy and what they went through," Samantha said, her voice strained.

"The kidnapper has privileged information about their psychological makeup," Earl said.

"It must be to do with those therapists," Julian said, rising from his chair. "They messed with their heads. Who else would know?"

"This is not about what happened between you and Felicity or anyone else," Samantha said. "This is about finding Michael and Abby."

"Then look at the therapists. They made up this fantasy."

"You're a bloody liar."

Samantha slapped him, putting her shoulder into it. Julian stood there, his face burning, his eyes filled with fury as his right eye twitched.

"Your tic gives you away. It's the only honest thing about you, a tiny little saboteur of an adulterer."

"Once and for all, what happened between Felicity and me happened once," Julian said. "There was nothing weird going on. Straight sex, that's all. Michael and Abby saw nothing. All this stuff about sadomasochism and spiders and snakes is fiction. The therapists put it into their heads. I think they're behind this. And both of them or one of them has hired the kidnapper."

"Why would they do that?"

"Money, Samantha. You know how alluring it is."

"Julian, I'm sick of your lies."

"It is not a lie."

"You keep saying it to me, and each time it sounds more and more ridiculous."

"I admit I slept with Felicity. The rest is fabrication. I think Ruby and Wakefield deliberately planted those ideas in their minds as a prelude to this. They're a pair of con artists."

"If Michael and Abby didn't walk in on you, how did they know?"

"They didn't. Maybe they heard a phone conversation and guessed. Maybe in therapy it came up and the therapists exaggerated it. But no one walked in on it. Felicity?"

"I'm tired of talking about it," Felicity said.

"But you did used to keep spiders and snakes," Greg said.

She shrugged her shoulders. "They may have gone into that room without us knowing."

Julian waved his hand at Samantha. "There. You've slept with me. Have I ever wanted to tie you up?"

"No, Julian, but you do like hurting people," Samantha said.

"This whole kidnapping is about money. I think when Michael and Abby went into therapy Ruby and Wakefield did their research on me, then decided to screw up our kids."

"But the therapy helped them."

"No, the therapy put me in the frame for something I didn't do, while the therapists planned the kidnapping."

"This isn't going to get our children back."

"We'll find out who's behind this."

Samantha sat down and turned her back to him.

"We must keep our personal resentments out of this," Greg said. "We've already angered this man. He wants money. Julian, it's down to you."

"I know it is."

Julian slammed his tumbler down on a mahogany table, cracking the glass, and spilling whiskey across the wood and onto the floor. He'd cut his finger and he put it to his mouth, his lips running with blood, his eyes feral and alive. He walked out of the room. Felicity was standing by the door, and he pushed her out of the way. As he did, his hand brushed her breasts, leaving a red smear on her dress. She grabbed the handle of the door to stop herself from falling.

Samantha walked over to her and looked at the stain. "You've never admitted it to me, even though we all know it happened. Greg won't talk about it, as if he's trying to protect your honor. Julian lies. You were my friend."

"What do you want from me?"

"Admit what you did with my husband."

"I don't think Julian likes any of us anymore. We're such a strange crowd. I wonder what Earl makes of us and our fragile façade."

"Earl's an onlooker in this sick drama. You need the illusion you're desired and undetected, don't you, Felicity?"

"I don't think I understand. You're being too deep for me."

"Everyone in this room knows you and Julian were having an affair. They know about the kinky sex, and your need for punishment. But if you admitted it to me, you'd lose something, wouldn't you, as if you want the affair to continue because it makes you feel so soiled and cleansed at the same time?"

"You're losing me, Samantha."

"There's something else, something we don't know."

"You mean that I'm the spider woman?"

"You used to tell me things about yourself. You call

yourself a whore, yet you need absolution. You seek the pain in pleasure and, in my filthy lying husband, you've found the perfect fuck."

"My, my, that's some analysis," Felicity said, her voice filled with barely suppressed hostility.

"Greg, haven't you anything to say?" Samantha asked. "I know what happened, so do you, yet you maintain this silence."

Greg leaned forward in his chair and shook his head. Felicity was swaying as she walked toward him, trying to move in a dignified manner, trying to convince them she was unscathed.

But when she got to him, she slumped into the chair next to him and turned her face to his, her expression imploring him for some unspoken need as she stared at his unyielding profile.

"We're all supporting Julian's lies," Samantha said.

Just then Julian returned, smoothing a plaster on his finger. He glared at Samantha. "The support in this marriage all comes from me," he said. Then he turned his face away from her in disgust and walked straight over to Earl. "I can have the money tomorrow. What will you do?"

"Drop if off, and ask for Michael and Abby to be released."

"But we can't communicate with his man."

"When he asks for it to be delivered, tell him he'll get half the cash and the rest when he hands them over."

CHAPTER 22

Abby wet herself as she watched the snakes. This time there was no cover on the box, she could see them writing inside.

The kidnapper held it in front of her. "Next time, you're naked."

Then he climbed up onto Michael's cage, unlocked it, and dropped them in one by one. Abby turned her back and began to scream. Then she heard him punching the front of her cage.

"Watch them, Abby, watch the sliding penises you're afraid of, or I'll put them next to your skin," he said.

She turned round and stared at them as Michael retreated to the far end of his cage.

"They're harmless," the kidnapper said. "They're

grass snakes, but I may place some venomous ones in your cage. Are you afraid of semen, Abby?"

Abby passed out as the kidnapper went inside Michael's cage, picked the snakes up one by one, and put them back in the box.

The Villas and Sheens got the film the next day. It was the same day Julian went missing.

Earl was returning to his flat at Digby Mansions in Hammersmith when Samantha called him. He rode straight there.

"The bastard has lied to me about everything," she said, handing him a note in the hallway.

It was written in blue ballpoint.

"'I haven't got the cash. I've been losing money left, right, and center for too long now, trying to keep it all afloat, I can't pay the ransom.'"

"You had no idea?" Earl said.

"None. I found out today that the house is heavily mortgaged, and he's defaulted on two payments."

"Then we ask Greg to come up with it."

"I can't get hold of Julian. I don't know where he is. His mobile goes straight to voicemail. And get this. I was going through his financial records. He was investing in a commercial property project that's fallen apart. He owes millions. He doesn't have anything in the bank."

"Sam, can I see those papers?"

She took him into Julian's office, a large, expensively furnished room that looked out onto the manicured lawns at the back of the house. It presented an image of a success that was now merely historical. Julian's desk was covered in bank statements. Earl spent the next two hours looking through them all. It was six p.m. when he came across the name Norman Jones.

"This doesn't look good," he said to Samantha. "I remember this case. Norman Jones worked for Newham Council. Julian was investing in a commercial project in the Docklands. That was where he lost all the money. The project had problems from the start. Jones tried to block several things Julian was trying to push through. It seems bribes were being given. Julian won the first round. But his plans were too environmentally unfriendly, and Norman successfully stopped the project for two months, in which Julian began to lose money. I read about what happened next in the papers."

"What happened?" Samantha said.

"Norman was found dead. He'd been shot at his office, a professional hit."

"You think Julian contracted it?"

"It seems likely."

"Do you think this is what's behind the kidnapping?"

"It's got to be connected."

"So what happened to the project?"

"The building company Julian had hired, and which had been kept waiting for two months, went bust. Julian struggled to find a replacement. It was a huge job and the major contractors were involved in other projects. His debt was large by then, and another council official began to investigate, blocking his efforts to get the project back on schedule. But there's another key player in here, the architect."

"Greg?"

"Right. It seems Greg had also piled a load of money into the project. He is as liable as Julian. Their combined debts amount to some two hundred million pounds. I would estimate that Greg is bankrupt. We have two men maintaining the pretence of wealth while their world crumbles. They each have a child who's been kidnapped."

"Earl, what is going on?"

"I don't know, but if Julian hired a hit man he couldn't pay, that could have led to the kidnapping."

"What are you going to do?"

"Talk to Greg. There's no way he could have come up with two million in cash."

CHAPTER 23

Felicity was out when Earl parked the Ninja outside the Sheens' Richmond home. Greg answered the door.

"I wasn't expecting you," he said, looking over Earl's shoulder into the street.

"May I have a word?"

"Come in." Greg took him into his study. A bottle of Courvoisier sat on his desk. "Drink?"

"No thanks," Earl said.

"Has there been a development?" Greg said, pouring cognac into a glass.

"Julian's disappeared."

"You mean he's been kidnapped?"

"I think that's unlikely."

"Has he come up with the money?"

"He can't, as I'm sure you know."

"Earl, you're losing me."

"Does the name Norman Jones ring any bells?"

Greg set his glass down. "Yes, it does as a matter of fact."

"You were involved in the project, weren't you?"

"You mean the one in Docklands?"

"Yes. Did you know that Julian took out a hit on Norman Jones?"

"You mean he had him assassinated?"

"We're running out of time. I think Abby and Michael's kidnapping has to do with the man Julian hired."

Greg sat down heavily at his desk. "He messed the whole thing up."

"Who did?"

"Julian. He involved me in a disastrous financial situation and then refused to bail me out."

"He hasn't got the money."

"I don't believe that. Julian owns properties all over London."

"I've just been looking at his finances, and they're not good."

"Has he come up with the money for the ransom?"

"No. How did you manage to get two million together, when you're about to lose everything?"

"I don't know where you get that idea from."

"The papers I was looking at in Julian's office. Two

hundred million owing on the project. Your name's all over it."

"I had some capital."

"You're lying."

"I think you ought to leave."

"Can you raise another two million to pay off the kidnapper?"

"Yes."

"And let me inspect the contents of the bag?"

"What?"

"I didn't last time."

"From what I can see, Earl, you've failed to get my daughter back. I'll deal with the kidnapper from here."

"You don't want me to see, do you? Did you stuff it with blank paper?"

"Why would I do that?"

"Because you have no capital. I've seen the bank statements. You don't even have enough money to pay for that bottle of brandy."

Greg opened his mouth and moved his lips, then put his glass to them. "The whole thing's Julian's fault."

"You mean the affair with Felicity? How did you feel about it when you found out?"

"How do you think I bloody felt?"

"And you were going bankrupt at the same time. It must have been a rough few weeks."

"You don't know the half of it."

"Why don't you tell me?"

"Why don't you get hold of Julian and get him to cough up, then we can get our children back? I never want to speak to the man again, let alone sit in the same room as him."

"You must hate him. He destroyed your marriage."

"What do you think?"

"Do you hate Felicity too?"

There was a picture of her on a table next to his desk, and Greg glanced at it. She was younger, and smiling at the camera. "I loved the fucking bitch."

"This is all about the affair, isn't it?"

"I don't know, ask Julian."

"I can't, he's disappeared."

"Well, find him. That's what you're good at, isn't it? Find Abby."

"How can I without your help?"

"My help?"

"Greg, you have no money. Julian has none either. Whoever kidnapped your children is going to kill them if he isn't paid."

"Do you think I don't know that?"

"Who did Julian hire to get Norman killed?" Earl said.

"Norman has nothing to do with this."

"How do you know?"

Greg put his forefingers against his temples and lowered his head. Earl waited for him to speak. He thought Greg was considering his response until he saw something splash the blotter on his desk. Then Greg raised his head and Earl saw he was crying.

"It was me. I hired the kidnapper."

CHAPTER 24

Greg hadn't heard the front door open, nor had he seen Felicity standing at the door as he made the confession. His eyes pooled with tears as he lifted his glass and emptied it. Felicity walked over to him, and he raised his face to hers. He looked like a schoolboy who'd been caught stealing and now faced punishment.

"You hired someone to kidnap and torture our daughter?" she said.

"Not to torture her."

"But you paid this man to abduct her?"

"Yes."

She slapped him, knocking his glass onto the carpet. "Why, you bastard? Why take it out on Abby?"

"I'm in debt, thanks to Julian."

"So you use our daughter to pay your way out?"

"It's not as simple as that, is it?" Greg dried his eyes and stood up. He went over to a cabinet and removed another glass. "Anyone else?"

Earl shook his head.

"Do you think this is the time for drinks?" Felicity said.

"Go and talk to Julian, ask him why we're about to lose everything."

"I'm asking you."

"And here I am, thinking you prefer his company, especially when you have his cock in your hand and he's holding a whip. What kind of fucking whore are you?"

"The kind of fucking whore who wants her daughter back. Pay this man, tell him to release her."

"I can't."

"What do you mean you can't?"

"I don't have any money, get Julian to pay."

"Okay, fine."

She picked up the phone.

"Julian is bankrupt," Earl said.

"What?"

"He and Greg have lost a huge amount of money."

"He's got the money," Greg said.

"Then why do you think he won't come up with it?"

"Maybe he doesn't like his son. He always bullied him."

"No, Greg, Julian has nothing," Earl said.

Greg turned to Felicity as she put the phone down. "He lied about everything, about the investment, about you and him, he even lied when Abby's therapist found out why she was so screwed up. He was trying to get me involved in another deal, covering up how much debt he was in. He said he'd sold some assets that were worth millions. He's probably still fucking you."

"He's not," Felicity said.

"Why don't you take your clothes off and let us see if you've got any marks on your back?"

"Greg, stop it."

"I'm sure you wouldn't mind stripping in front of Earl. How cheap you are."

"Greg, we need to make contact with the kidnapper," Earl said. "If there's no money to pay him, you're going to have to call it off."

"I can't."

"What do you mean?"

"I can't reach him."

"Since when?" Earl said.

"Since yesterday. He called me and said if he wasn't paid by tomorrow, he was going to start the killings. He said he was getting rid of his mobile, that it was too risky."

"He'll make contact?"

"He said he'd call me today. If he doesn't get the money by midnight tomorrow, he says he'll torture and kill Abby and Michael."

"You bastard," Felicity said. She launched herself at

him and began punching him. "Why did you do this to our daughter?"

Greg grabbed her wrists and threw her against the fireplace. "Because she's not our daughter, is she?"

Felicity had banged her head and stood very still. "What are you talking about?"

"She's Julian's."

"She's yours."

"What a week that was, when it all came out, more bad news than a man can cope with, me knowing I was going bankrupt, the therapeutic revelations about Abby's mental state and you being the cause. And Julian kept lying. I could handle the idea of an affair all those years ago. I loved you, you bitch. I knew I was going bust. You'd gone shopping to buy some new shoes, my shallow corrupt wife, another man's whore, on a spending spree. I tried to be reasonable. I've always been a reasonable man. But this thought kept nagging at me, what if your affair had been going on a lot longer? What if all those times I was away on business, you and Julian had been fucking? Or what if he was one of many men?"

"He wasn't."

"Well, I got a DNA test carried out. I made a decision, if Abby was my daughter I'd stay with you. If she wasn't, then I was going to get as much money as possible and leave you."

"Abby's your daughter. I was careful."

"So you were seeing him before she was born?"

"Yes."

"Well, you weren't careful enough. Abby is not my daughter. I decided to get the paternity test carried out during the time Julian was trying to cover it all up and sending both Abby and Michael to the hypnotherapist. That should have told me everything. He knows, doesn't he? That's why he paid for her."

"No, he doesn't. I don't."

Felicity's eyes were empty, as if some implosion had occurred in her being. She tried to walk toward a chair and collapsed.

Earl lifted her gently onto the sofa.

"Her head's bleeding," he said. He looked over at the fireplace and saw a strand of her hair stuck to the marble ledge.

"I remember the day I got the result telling me just what a cuckold I am, you were talking to Abby. She was asking why Julian was paying for the hypnotherapy and you said, 'Daddy pays for a lot.' I thought, yes, I do, I've paid for you throughout this fucking marriage, and I'm not paying for you anymore. I figured a million would see me though my final days. I agreed to split the two million with the kidnapper. Except I didn't know Julian was bankrupt. Once again, he lied."

"What did you put in the bag the night you left me behind at the warehouse?" Earl said.

"Blank paper, quite appropriate isn't it?"

"Well, you've misled all of us."

"You've walked into the middle of something, Earl, I'm sure it's happened to you before."

"Julian must have known how much debt you're in, how did you convince him you had two million?"

"When I sold my accountancy practice, I had a lot of assets, Julian thinks I still have them."

"And why is that?" Felicity asked.

"Because I told him I do."

"You're each as bad as the other, competing about your wealth when you don't have it."

"I didn't tell him I'd sunk everything into the property venture after I'd found out about him and you. I didn't want to give him the satisfaction of knowing he'd ruined me twice. I am nothing like Julian. I don't go round fucking other men's wives."

"Right now, Abby and Michael will get killed if you don't do something to stop it," Earl said. "Is that what you want?"

"No, of course not."

"Then you have to call the whole thing off when he rings."

"He won't have it. The man's unhinged. Snakes and spiders. I never asked him to do that. I told him to kidnap them, film them, and then let them go."

"When are you expecting to hear from him?"

"He could call any time."

"Where is he holding them?"

"I don't know."

"How does he know about their phobias?"

"He read Abby's notes."

"You got him to burgle Marion Wakefield's office?"

"It was during the time Julian kept saying the therapists were charlatans. The pathetic thing is I wanted to believe him. You know I'd tied so much capital in with him, I thought if he's right and it is a load of claptrap...isn't that Julian's word for the truth?...then nothing has changed. My marriage is still what I thought it was. I needed to find out what Abby had said to her therapist."

"Who did you hire to kidnap them?"

"His name's Two Pence."

"How did you meet him?"

"Julian introduced me to Micky Fallow. I was at the office late one night drawing up some designs. Julian told me what Norman was up to, and that he was arranging for him to be removed. I thought he meant sacked. You come up against these council officials all the time. They're a pain in the arse, small-minded bureaucrats who have no idea of design. It was late one Friday night. We were all drinking whiskey. Fallow is not the sort of chap you want to mess with, clearly criminal. Julian handed him a case—full of money. I imagine. Fallow said, 'That'll take care of it,' then he looked at me and said, 'We all got to keep quiet.' I wanted Norman out of the way. I didn't know Julian was going to get him killed."

"Micky Fallow is an extremely dangerous man," Earl said.

"You know him?"

"I know his reputation for extortion, racketeering, breaking people's legs, and getting them killed."

"What have you got involved with?" Felicity said.

"None of this would have happened if you'd kept your cunt in your panties," Greg said.

He tipped his glass of cognac over her head.

"Greg, enough," Earl said. "How did you meet this guy Two Pence?"

"When I discovered Abby wasn't my daughter, I called Micky Fallow. I found his number in Julian's phone. I asked him if he did burglaries. He said 'No, but I know someone who does.' He arranged for me to meet this man. I was to walk into Richmond Park by the gate on the hill at eight, after it was closed to cars, and walk for two hundred yards left, away from the gate. I waited for him to show, not knowing who to look for. Finally, he turned up and said, 'You Micky's mate?'"

"What does he look like?"

"Tall, well built, doesn't say much."

"Is that all?"

"He was wearing a hood and shades."

"What information did you give him?"

"I gave him the therapist's address and told him I wanted the file on Abby Sheen. I also instructed him to take more than one file."

"And you hired him to kidnap Abby and Michael?"

"When I met him in the park, he told me he'd done

this sort of thing before and knew what he was doing, he added, 'break-ins, kidnappings, I'm your man.' He gave me his mobile number. When I got the DNA test back, I called him. I told him I wanted two people kidnapped, that it would only take a few days for the money to come through and how did he fancy sharing two million with me? He wanted to know why I was hiring him to kidnap my own daughter. I told him to remove suspicion from myself, and explained that Julian Villa was a wealthy man."

"And you don't have any other information about him?" Earl said.

"No."

"Well, if you didn't instruct him to lock them in glass cages and put snakes and spiders in them, it seems your kidnapper has decided to have some fun."

"What does that mean?"

"It means you haven't hired a run-of-the-mill kidnapper, but someone with deep psychological problems."

"He's going to torture my daughter and kill her," Felicity said.

"What are you going to do, Earl?" Greg asked.

"When he calls, you say you've got the money. I'll have to ambush him and, this time, I'll have to hurt him, it's the only way of getting Abby and Michael back."

"And what if you can't catch him? He got away from you the last time."

"I was trying to tail him, this time I won't be."

"What are you going to do? Take him somewhere

and beat it out of him?" Just then Greg's phone rang on his desk. He picked it up and looked at caller ID. "Private call, it could be him."

"Answer it," Earl said. "Tell him you have the money and arrange for a drop-off point."

As Greg answered, Earl and Felicity could hear the caller's voice.

"Hello?" Greg said.

"You got the money?"

"I have."

"All of it?"

"Yes."

"All right, drop it off in a bag. There's a small outbuilding behind the second warehouse in Royal Park, the one past where you left the paper. It's got peeling blue paint on it and a broken window. Put the bag inside the building. You can fit it through the window. Leave it there tomorrow at midnight."

"I want Abby and Michael back. Will you hand them over?"

"Once I got the money. And no funny business, don't bring anyone this time."

"I told you I didn't know about him. Julian Villa hired him."

"There are some more films in the post, just so you know I mean business."

CHAPTER 25

Earl rode the Ninja away from Richmond and the ruined house full of antiques and faded lies, all the way to Samantha. She answered the door in a pair of track suit bottoms and a T-shirt. She'd been working out.

Sweat had formed in a patch on her chest, and the outline of her breasts was clear against the wet cotton. Earl stood there for a moment without saying anything, remembering how they used to be in bed, then she laid her hand on his arm.

"There's still no word from Julian," she said.

"I have some news, Sam."

She took him up to the kitchen and made fresh coffee as he told her about Greg hiring the kidnapper. Samantha

sat there, saying little, as he described the row between
Greg and Felicity.

"Julian has caused this, I blame him," she said, "but
Greg is fucking insane to have contracted a man he
knows nothing about, even if he hates Abby."

"Find Julian. he needs to speak to Micky Fallow."

"What are you going to do?"

"Find out who Two Pence is."

She placed her head on his chest. Earl looked into
her eyes then he took her face in his hands and her mouth
with his. He could feel the firmness of her breasts and her
pounding heart. Then they were alone in her bedroom
with the curtains drawn, and he knew her again, naked
beneath him, her body soft and pliant, her legs wrapped
around his waist, drawing him inside her, back to the
past, before Julian came along. She locked her ankles
around his waist as he moved her to a long and golden
ecstasy.

Samantha's eyes were wet as she lay beside him in
the gathering twilight, but her heart was his again, as if
they'd never been apart, and Julian was an aberration
from a nightmare. She touched his body with her finger-
tips, tracing lines she used to know each waking morning
all those years ago before he'd rise and go to work. Then
she craved him again, pushing thoughts of the glass house
away as she took him in her hand, guiding his hardness
inside her body.

"Fill me," she said, "take me away from this empti-
ness."

He knew how to touch her. He'd always known, and she considered that was part of the problem, an early teenage fear of losing something that gave her so much pleasure. But she took her pleasure now as she had another orgasm that was long and intense and allowed her to forget.

She waited for him. Earl took her nipples his mouth as he slowly worked his way toward his climax, then she felt him quiver inside her as he came. And she saw herself there in the dazzling emerald fire of his eyes, locked in physical desire, her face beautiful in his gaze.

"The years have been empty without you," she said.

"You're still that stunning teenager I felt high on."

"I'm older now, and wiser."

"Do you think we can give it another shot?"

She touched his face as she held him inside her. "Find my son Earl."

ℓↄℓↄ

As they made love, Felicity sat in her bedroom, weeping while Greg packed a case. He threw his clothes inside, his back to her.

"Where do you think you're going?" she said.

"Anywhere, away from you and this wreck of a life."

"No, you're not. You've got my daughter."

"You try stopping me."

She got up and began to hit him. Greg threw her

across the room and continued packing. Felicity picked up a lamp and smashed him across his head. Greg fell against a chair and lay there, his head bleeding. Then Felicity began to sob, her shoulders rising and falling, as she leaned down and touched his face.

"I'm sorry, it's all my fault," she said.

"You're damn right it is."

CHAPTER 26

While the fireworks went off, Julian was in his office. He'd slept there the night before on the sofa in the reception area, and now as he opened a bottle of Jim Beam, he heard the door open.

"Evening, Julian."

"Micky."

Micky Fallow was six foot, scarred, and had the lean muscle of a military man. He wore a cashmere coat and black leather gloves. Behind him, a large man with a boxer's face loomed in the door way. Julian could smell cigar smoke and aftershave as Micky walked slowly over to him and laid his hand on his shoulder.

"Dear oh dear, has it come to this?" he said, glancing at the whiskey bottle.

"I've lost everything. I need to borrow two million from you."

"Two million?"

"My son's been kidnapped."

"Has he?"

"So has Greg's daughter."

"Funny that."

"There nothing funny about it. I haven't got the money to pay the kidnapper."

"You never were very smart, were you, Julian?"

"You don't understand. If I don't come up with the money, my son will be killed."

"You think Greg is innocent, do you?"

"Innocent of what?"

"He asked me a few weeks ago if I knew a burglar. What's he up to?"

"A burglar?"

"Yes, I put him onto Two Pence, who also likes kidnapping. My guess is Greg's up to no good. But it ain't none of my business. Anyway, I ain't come here to chat."

"Two Pence?"

"Yes, you don't want to fuck around with him, do you, Kobbler?"

"No, you don't," the man at the door said in a booming voice.

"What are you saying?"

"I ain't saying nothing."

"Greg hired a burglar?"

"I ain't come here about Two Pence, but a lot more. You owe me, remember, that hit earned interest."

"I haven't got it."

"Oh dear, those are not the words I wanted to hear."

"Give me more time."

"No."

Micky winked at Kobbler and turned his back as Kobbler marched over to Julian and poured himself a whiskey. Then he pulled a Luger from his pocket and shot Julian in the head.

The shot knocked Julian backward onto his desk. Micky straightened his tie in the lift.

CHAPTER 27

The films arrived the following morning. Samantha watched the man in the hood hold a box up to the camera. He turned the camera away from himself and focused it on Michael. Then the angle became elevated as he climbed the ladder and she saw an aerial shot of her son's cage. He tipped the tarantulas in, and Samantha listened to Michael's screams. He became frenetic. He punched the glass until his knuckles bled. Then he had a fit. He collapsed and the camera zoomed in on his shaking legs and the thick strand of saliva that dangled from his mouth. That is where the film ended.

Felicity watched a film in which the kidnapper tortured her daughter. He reminded her of Julian all those years ago as he stung her naked buttocks with a whip, his

expression hidden behind the hood. And it occurred to
Felicity that was what she enjoyed, not knowing how
much she was arousing a man, making him her sexual
priest, a faceless lover who would enjoy her body and
hurt her for it, using pain to wash the guilt away. The sig-
nal proof of Julian's arousal she'd received that night that
lay behind the phobias like a record of her sin, was the
semen that gushed from his erect penis as she took him in
her hand and found intense satisfaction in watching his
seed explode from him, as if her touch made him lose
control. Then she saw the anger in his eyes and turned to
see the two children standing at the door. They caused a
coitus interruptus that bred the discontent that spread like
a polluted tide across both families. She'd never got fin-
ish the act with Julian that night, never reached her sin-
ner's climax, and it seemed to her she'd searched and
hungered for it ever since. That was why the affair had
continued for so long. She resented Samantha for the fact
that Julian stayed with her. Samantha misunderstood Julian. He gave Felicity intense pleasure of a kind that re-
deemed her sense of deep depravity. The glass house re-
flected her affair, and her sexual prison. And she wondered, as these thoughts flickered into her mind like the
tail of a snake, whether she felt real guilt at all.

Now she watched as the kidnapper entered Abby's
cage and stripped her. Abby fought, but he was too
strong. He tore her blouse from her, forced her to the
floor, and undid her jeans. Her face was turned away

from him, lost in humiliation, her eyes wandered from the glass house to a memory or thought that would hold her broken mind together like a drop of glue. She kicked and struggled, but he held her down on the glass floor with one hand around her throat as he cut off her bra, dragged her jeans off, and sliced her panties from her body with a filleting knife, nicking her skin as she moved.

"Careful, we don't want you bleeding just yet," he said.

Felicity honed in on the voice and tried to paint a face to match it, but he remained unknowable, distant from the world of emotions that tumbled inside her like jagged rocks.

The kidnapper looked at Abby's naked body, running his eyes across her skin.

"Get off me, you fucking pervert," she said.

"Natural blonde, I see. Don't scare Michael with your pubic hair. I like a bit of bush myself. I'll enjoy seeing to you later after the snakes have crawled all over you."

He stood up and kicked her clothes away to the far corner of her cage as Abby got to her feet, covering her breasts.

"Don't be shy," he said, pulling her arms away.

"I'll kill you if you lay a hand on me."

"Will you? Your therapist said you hate sex and men. Was it a shock seeing your mother getting whipped?"

"How do you know all this?"

He left the cage and tipped the box of snakes inside it. Abby pressed herself against the glass to get away from them, but they were too numerous. One of them began to crawl up her leg and she kicked it away. It hit the wall with a sound like meat slapping metal and slid across the floor. Abby was shaking and tried to jump up to the open roof. She fell and landed on a snake. The final shot was of Abby screaming as one of them curled around her upper thigh.

When the film ended, Felicity went straight into the spare room where Greg had slept after being unable to find his car keys, which she had hidden.

"See what the man you hired is doing to Abby," she said, throwing the film on the bed.

In Kensington, Samantha poured herself a large vodka and dialed Julian's mobile number.

"I don't know where you are, you bastard, but you better get back here."

CHAPTER 28

Leonard stood in a well-to-do road in Richmond and watched as Francis Truman came out of a large Victorian house into his front garden and loaded some bags into the back of his Jeep. As Truman drove away, he didn't see Leonard, who was standing at the mouth of a passage that ran beside a house on the opposite side of the road.

Leonard waited a while, looking at Truman's house, then he left the road. He walked several blocks to the station, where he got a train to Surrey, and then walked to Harry's house.

Harry answered the door. He let Leonard in and took him through to the kitchen where Mandy was making breakfast.

"Got some bacon on, Len," she said. "You ain't shaved."

"I ain't hungry, Mandy."

"Come on, Len, have some grub," Mandy said.

"No, I'll just have a coffee."

"Suit yourself."

"I've come to see Mum."

"She's upstairs," Harry said.

Mandy poured Leonard a cup of coffee, and he went upstairs to see Mary. She was sitting in a chair by the window, reading the *Daily Express*.

"How's he treating you?" he said, kissing her on the cheek.

"Very well, thank you."

"Nice room."

"Isn't it a pretty view?"

"When I've done up my gaff, you can move in with me."

"I don't need to move no more, Leonard."

"You'll like the house."

"I think I'll stay here."

He hid his frustration from his mother and talked to her for an hour, glancing out of the window from time to time at the large garden, and Mandy hanging washing out. When he left, Mandy was downstairs checking her lipstick in the mirror.

"Harry's gone out, want to stay for lunch?" she said.

"No thanks."

"We used to get on. What's up with you?"

"I don't think Harry wants me here."

"Don't say that."

"I think he knows about what happened."

"How can he know?"

"The way you look at me, Mandy, he's always watching you when you're around me."

CHAPTER 29

Micky Fallow was less than pleased with the financial situation Julian Villa had left behind him. The day that Earl was readying himself for the second drop-off, Fallow's chauffeur, Knuckles, eased his black Bentley to a stop outside the house in Kensington that Samantha, unbeknownst to her, now owned. He sat there smoking a Cuban cigar in the back seat, brushing a piece of ash as light as a feather from the collar of his cashmere coat as he estimated the property's worth.

"I'd say ten mill, Knuckles, what do you think?" Fallow said, his lips rounded on the butt of the cigar.

"I'd say at least, Micky."

"I think I'll call in the debt."

"Why not, Micky, why not?" Knuckles said, his enormous shoulders rising and falling as he chuckled.

Knuckles almost always chuckled when Micky mentioned the word debt, anticipating action. For Knuckles was only a part-time chauffeur. The rest of his time in Micky's employment, he spent beating and chaining up Micky's enemies. Knuckles specialised in hanging men upside down at the meat factory Micky owned in the East End. He enjoyed punching them, aiming his fists at their organs, as they turned blue. If any women got in Micky's way, he got Kobbler to shoot them. That was what he was for. Kobbler was good with guns, Knuckles with his fists. For Micky, each person had a special use, and if anyone strayed outside his role, he was not a happy man. And Micky hated not to feel happy. It affected his calm, neutral expression, rugged good looks, easy manner, and dead eyes. Happiness consisted in damaging anyone who got in his way in a relaxed business-like manner. Any woman who owed him money ended up with her brains on her blotter, because Micky thought a bruised woman was an unattractive sight. But the men—that involved something else. Torture, in all its glorious forms, was a TV show for Micky. Women who did what they were told were another matter. They had their own uses.

"That fellow, the one Kobbler shot, he owed you," Knuckles said, turning round in the seat and looking at Micky.

"He did."

"This is your house then?"

"It is mine, old son, and all that's in it—hello."

Just then Samantha came out of the front door, wearing a blue wool skirt and matching jacket. As she walked toward her Mercedes in high heels, Micky ran his eyes down her body, licked his lips, and pulled a piece of stray tobacco from his tongue. He watched Samantha get in the car and drive away.

"I'll have a piece of that," he said.

"I bet you will, Micky," Knuckles said.

As the Bentley moved through Kensington, drifting past the palace and into the city, where Micky had some debtors he was visiting that day, Samantha drove straight to Julian's office. She parked in the basement garage and took the lift to his floor. She opened the glass door and passed through the empty reception area. Then she entered his office.

At first she thought he was sleeping, and she felt a flicker of anger that he was supine on his desk, a bottle of whiskey by him. While she tried to get her son back, he'd come here to get drunk. Then she saw the blood spatter on the carpet and his head, and she began to scream. She called Earl on her mobile in the hall, her legs hollow as she left the building.

CHAPTER 30

Abby sat in the corner of her cage, her knees against her chest, her face buried in them. Michael stood at the front of his cage banging on the glass to get her attention.

"We need to get out of here," he said.

She raised her head and got to her feet then wandered slowly to the vent.

"How are we going to do that?"

"The next time he comes in, I'm going to attack him., If he turns his back, I can grab him. All it takes is for me to get out then we can both get up that ladder."

"You've seen how strong he is."

"What else can we do, wait for him to kill us? I don't understand why my father hasn't paid. What is going on?"

"There's something we don't know about, something to do with what our therapists told us."

"He knows about what we saw."

"Do you think there was someone else involved in what went on between my mother and your father?"

"Who?"

"I don't know, maybe one of them had an affair with someone else's husband or wife," Abby said. "Maybe that's why we've been kidnapped."

"Revenge?"

"It could be."

CHAPTER 31

At eight p.m. Earl followed Greg to the second warehouse in Royal Park. He decided to get there early, in case they were being watched. Greg found the outbuilding and inserted the bag stuffed with blank paper through the broken window, then drove away as Earl took up a position on top of the building. It was a short drop to the ground, and he intended to jump the kidnapper.

He waited in the silence and the growing cold of the night. The sky was blue, and he could see the area clearly. He estimated there were two ways the kidnapper would come for his money, either using the path he and Greg had used or from the opposite end of the warehouse. As midnight approached, Earl got his blackjack out of his pocket.

Another hour crawled by. Then he heard the bike. It was a small engine dirt bike, and it was coming fast from the other side of the warehouse. Earl watched as it approached then stopped below him. The rider got off. He had a helmet on and Earl couldn't see his face. As he reached in for the bag, Earl jumped him, knocking him to the ground. Earl could hear that he was winded as he struck him across the arm with the blackjack. He reached down to pull off his helmet but the kidnapper performed a leg sweep, and Earl found himself on his back.

Then the kidnapper was standing over him. He punched Earl in the face. Earl swung out with his blackjack, cracking it against his ankle. The snap of metal on bone reverberated in the empty enclosure. Earl got to his feet and aimed a punch at the man's solar plexus but his fist was blocked, and the kidnapper elbowed him in the face. Earl felt blood trickling onto his lips as he grabbed the man around the throat. He had a tight grip on him and tried to see his eyes beneath the helmet, but the kidnapper punched him hard in the stomach.

Then he began to throw one punch after the other, forcing Earl to lose his grip as he swung both arms up and outward, breaking Earl's stranglehold. Earl caught him twice on the arm with the blackjack, but he kept up his rhythm, his fists pounding Earl, until eventually he knocked him to the ground. Earl saw him stand above him beneath the cold blue sky, throw the bag over his shoulder, and get on the bike. Then he was gone. Earl stumbled to the road and his Ninja.

CHAPTER 32

As the kidnapper rode away, Greg was sitting in his office with Felicity. The fire was on and his face looked more flushed than usual.

"This is the last bottle," he said, pouring them both a cognac. "Enjoy it. I don't know if I'll have the cash in a few days to get another one."

"It can't be that bad."

"It is. Julian screwed me up in more ways than one."

"We have to get Abby back. You're her father."

"Except I'm not, am I?"

"You brought her up. I saw your face when you watched what that man is doing to her."

"I never wanted her hurt. I thought he'd keep her a few days, and I'd get the money. I was so angry I wanted to hurt Julian. And you."

"I don't blame you for being angry. But Abby."

"All right. I've told you I'll do what I can to get her out of there, but what if Earl isn't successful?"

"Do you think he'll kill her?"

"I have to find a way to get through to him."

"You do want to see Abby again?"

"Of course I do."

"So what do we do now?"

"Wait for Earl to turn up."

CHAPTER 33

When Samantha called Earl from Julian's office, he was about to leave for the second drop off. She found consolation in his voice and drove home, where she drank half a bottle of Sauvignon Blanc then called the police. Officers DI Keith Greaves and PC Hank Rafter arrived at her house and spent an hour talking to her. Greaves was tall and had an angry scar running across his cheek. Samantha kept gazing at the disfiguration, as if ugliness held sway in her mind. Rafter was a smaller man, who sat awkwardly in a chair with his hands tucked neatly into his pockets.

"Would you have any idea why someone would shoot your husband?" Greaves said.

"He owed money, as I've recently discovered."

"You think he was shot because of that?" Rafter said.

"Yes."

"Do you know who he owed money to?"

Samantha hesitated, thinking of the glass house. "I'm in shock as I'm sure you can understand."

"You think he was mixing with criminals?" Greaves said.

"My husband didn't tell me much."

"But you know he owed money."

She looked at Greaves and his scar and imagined what the kidnapper would do to Michael if she said the wrong thing. "That's all I know. I thought he was missing, and I went to his office."

"Where you found him with a bullet in his head."

"That's right."

"Not the sort of thing you run into every day, is it?"

"Look, Inspector, I'm reporting a crime. I don't know why someone would shoot my husband, he kept me in the dark."

"Wealthy man, was he?"

"Don't you think you ought to go and inspect his office?"

"Not our department, but the crime scene investigators will be round there now, don't worry, they'll get forensics," Greaves said, standing up.

She watched Rafter get up too then she showed them to the door.

When they left, they seemed to her an invasive personification of all she found vile, the small lost men, the scarred, and hopeless. And her body sought relevant beauty. As she thought of Earl, Julian's office was being sealed off by men in gloves and masks, whose eyes studied the murder with clinical detachment. Samantha drank wine and thought about what Earl had been doing that night. It was two a.m. when she heard his Ninja outside. She rose from bed naked, went downstairs, opened the door, and stood there with the moonlight falling across her body.

As Earl came into the hallway she touched his bleeding face.

"He got away again?" she said.

"Yes."

She went upstairs, washed his face, and bandaged the side of his head. Earl lay on her bed. She undid his trousers, took him between her thighs, and drew him deep inside her to the place where she felt like the same woman he'd made love to when they were young and before she knew the glass house existed. The act of making love was the only thing that shed the image of it from her mind.

Earl had his hands on her breasts as she felt his seed swimming inside her in the hungry dark.

As they lay there, she looked at him, this man who induced a sexual hunger in her that had no place in her marriage.

She thought of Julian pushing inside her as she stared

past him at the clock or a picture on the wall. She thought of how she'd tricked herself into marrying Julian, and how she desired money, but now she knew what she desired, and it was Earl and all his dark mystery.

Afterward, she talked about going to Julian's office.

"Tell me how you found him," Earl said.

"I went there to look for him. I was so angry, I wanted to scream at him for running out on me like that. I thought he was sleeping, then I saw the blood."

"I wish I'd been able to come to you then."

"You had to drop off the money."

"This guy can handle himself."

"There aren't many men who can beat you up."

"I think he's going to do something disastrous if I don't find him."

"What I hired you to do and what you are now involved in are two different things."

"Who do you think shot Julian?"

"Who knows? He had too many secrets."

"The man Greg hired came through Micky Fallow. I think Fallow got Julian killed and knows who's holding Michael and Abby."

"Are you going to talk to him?"

"I am, although I don't think Fallow is a man who parts with information without a price."

"I better get what I have together, which is not much."

"No one can meet the ransom money, and it's too late now."

"I have a few thousand."

CHAPTER 34

It was eight a.m. when Leonard went to visit his mother. Harry was leaving for work, and Leonard spent all morning with Mary, making her tea, chatting to her about the past. There was a glimmer in his eyes when he left, and, for a second, he forgot about the things that troubled him on a daily basis. Mandy was in the kitchen frying bacon as he came downstairs. She was wearing a pair of white jeans and a low-cut blue blouse. Leonard could smell fresh coffee as he stood in the hall watching her. He had his hand on the door and was about to leave when she turned round and saw him.

"Len, you're not going without saying goodbye, are you?" she said, coming out. She had a tea towel in her hand. She put it on the hall table, laid her other hand over his, and removed it from the door. "Have a sandwich with me, keep me company."

He sat there as she talked, of work, the past. The sandwich was good, the bacon crisp and the bread crusty, and it reminded him of her cooking. He stared through the window at the green lawn then at her face. He lowered his eyes briefly to the hint of her full cleavage that showed through the open button at the top of her blouse.

"You always did make a good sarny, Mandy."

"That's not the only tasty thing about me."

"Good bacon."

Mandy glanced at her cleavage. "Well, I've heard them called many things but not bacon before, Len."

"I don't think Harry would like you talking to me like that."

"Harry ain't here, is he, Len?"

"I better go."

"I think you need to relax more. Come on, I miss you."

"I'll have another rasher."

"I bet you will." Mandy got up and leaned down until her mouth was inches from Leonard's. Then she kissed him. "You can't fool me," she said.

They did it in the spare room, on white sheets that smelled of apricots. Leonard entered Mandy as she wrapped her legs around his waist, and the look on her face as she came was without a trace of guilt. Leonard studied it, knowing only guilt and secret pleasures he couldn't voice to the people in his diminished life. The pleasure he experienced was like the memory of a holiday. Then he saw Kenny's face again.

Afterward, as they lay there, he ran his hand across her taut buttocks and Mandy touched his face. He tried to find the old affection that he'd once known.

"We were always good together in bed," she said.

"I don't think Harry would like it."

"He don't have to know."

"You married him, Mandy."

"He gives me things."

"You mean he's got money."

"Don't say you didn't enjoy it."

"You wanted the money and that's why you married him."

CHAPTER 35

Abby and Michael hadn't been fed for twenty-four hours. Abby was shivering that morning, and Michael paced his cage.

"Someone has gone to great trouble to find out what went on in our therapy sessions," he said.

"My mother and your father have ruined our lives."

"And now our parents can't pay to get us out of here."

"Who would have access to our files?"

"The therapists."

"They can't be behind this," Abby said.

"Someone's been watching our lives."

"He wants money, Michael, that's what this is about."

"Then why this? Why torture us?"

"To put pressure on our parents."

"Or is it something else?"

"Like what?"

"Think of what happened after we had the therapy."

"You mean your father paying for us to go to the hypnotherapist?"

"He wants it covered up, but I know what I saw."

"And so do I."

"What if he's afraid of someone else finding out?"

"You mean another husband?"

"I think my father has many guilty secrets, and the kidnapper's using them."

CHAPTER 36

The clouds looked like torn cotton as the sun set that evening and Leonard waited at the mouth of the alley. He watched the lights come on in Pam Smythe's windows. He waited as shapes lost their edges and faded into darkness. He thought of Mandy and what they might have had if she hadn't chosen money over him, and his sense of arousal, as he thought of her in bed, turned into something sharp inside him. He moved out of the alley, into the street, entered the path that ran along the side of the house, and scaled the gate. He could see inside the kitchen. It was lit and empty. He landed without noise and tried the door. Then Leonard kicked it in.

Pam was in the living room, putting on makeup. She stopped as she heard the crash and went into the hall. She saw Leonard coming out of the kitchen and moved toward the phone, but he grabbed her by the arms and hoisted her off the floor. Pam tried to kick him, but Leonard threw her face down onto the carpet and pressed his body onto hers. He took a fistful of her hair and pushed her face into the shag pile, smearing it with rouge and lipstick. A strand of a saliva drooled out of Pam's mouth. He put his mouth close to her ear.

"I got some surprises for you, Pam, remember me?"

"Yes, you fucking creep, get off me."

"Getting ready to go out? Do you dress up for the doc?"

"You're a sick bastard."

"Am I?"

"My house mate will be back any minute."

"She's gone away. I done my research."

"My boyfriend's coming over."

"Don't tell lies, Pam. You only fuck doctors."

"You attacked the security guards, the police are after you."

"I can't hear what you're saying, you dumb bitch."

Her voice was muffled as Leonard pushed harder on the back of her head, mashing her teeth against her lips.

"Think about what you're doing," she said.

"I have."

"You're cutting my mouth."

"This is only the beginning."

Pam was dribbling pink saliva as Leonard yanked

her up by her hair. Then he put the bag over her head and her world went black.

CHAPTER 37

Micky Fallow had been thinking about Julian's wife since he'd watched her getting into her Mercedes. There was something about women and cars that was a turn on to him. Especially, if he bought them one and told them what to wear as they drove it. Especially, if they drove naked around the private grounds of his Surrey estate.

His wife, Anne, was a bleached blonde who ate pies when she was alone. Years of trying to maintain her weight for him and the barely hidden knowledge of his affairs forced her to alternate between drinking to block out her pain and indulging her taste for pastry, which was frequently.

Micky had business that took him away from home,

Anne didn't ask questions about his trips. She enjoyed the credit cards and shopping expeditions. As Micky made a call in his office that morning, she was dressing after her swim. She inspected her body in the mirror, touching her full breasts, feeling the implants Micky bought her for her forty-second birthday when middle age made its presence known too much for his liking.

Even in the right lights, she looked old, he'd said to her, but Micky was a generous guy. He paid for her to see the top surgeon. Then he enjoyed her enhanced figure. She'd looked great until then. He used to say she was in her late twenties. She was toned and always ready for him when he wanted it. She existed in his world as a private pleasure he controlled. Anne knew when to give him what he wanted. She had a Geiger counter locked on his moods. He was preoccupied today, she noticed. And when her husband was preoccupied, she stayed away.

As Anne dressed, Micky put down the phone. He'd instructed Knuckles on what to do and how to do it. He swung his handmade shoes on his desk and puffed at the ceiling, thinking of the blonde woman he'd acquired together with the house and other property owned by Julian Villa. He imagined her groaning under him in the back of his Bentley. He imagined all the things he'd do to her body. And she'd enjoy it.

The body was an amazing thing, and a means to get money. Inflicting pain on others got you cash, and cash bought you pleasure. Fallow thought of what Samantha would wear for him. He knew the kind of lingerie he wanted to remove from her. Julian Villa had left a debt. And Fallow was going to savor his wife.

❧❧❧

Samantha was sitting on the sofa in Greg's office as a man she had no knowledge of planned sexual acts with her. Earl was telling Greg and Felicity what had happened and Felicity was turning paler as he spoke. Greg looked hung over, his usual ruddy complexion now assuming an angry shade. Felicity stood up and fingered the top of her blouse. A vein throbbed in her neck.

"Earl, you have to save them."

"I need to speak to Micky Fallow," Earl said.

CHAPTER 38

Pam Smythe had no recollection of the journey that took her away from her home. When she opened her eyes, all she could see was a large wooden trunk and a pair of army boots on a concrete floor. She lifted her head and saw Mary Wells's son standing over her, dressed in an army uniform. He had his arms crossed as he picked her up from the floor, twisting his fist in her torn blouse. Her head was throbbing and the room went in and out of focus. But what she could see was that it was bare.

"Pam, I hoped to get you a nurse's uniform," he said, "but then you're not fit to wear one."

"Why are you doing this?"

"Because of the way you treated my mother."

"Look, I'm sorry, okay? I was having a hard day, but think about what you're doing."

"A hard day? See anyone killed, did ya?"

"Where am I?"

"You're in my place, Pam. Tell me, how does the doc do it to you?"

"I haven't slept with him."

"You'd like to, wouldn't you?"

"I have a boyfriend."

"I saw you at that pub do adjusting his tie."

"You've been following me."

"I always do my homework."

"Are you some kind of soldier?"

"That's right, Pam, that's what I am."

"They don't know who you are. I don't even know your name. Just let me walk away and that will be the end of the matter."

"Why would I let you walk away?"

"Because you don't want to go to prison."

"I ain't going to go to prison, Pam, no one will ever find you. Not here."

"I understand you're angry about your mother."

"You didn't that day when I complained to you."

"There are far worse hospitals than Kingston."

"And there are far better."

"Do you think, by doing this, it will change anything?"

"And what do you think I'm going to do?"

"I don't know, but I think you want to hurt me."

"Let me tell you about hurt, Pam. It's something you carry around inside you. It will change you."

"You mean it will scar me."

"That's right."

"You mother said you're a war hero."

"Funny, and I thought you didn't pay attention to what she said."

"Do you know what hours we do, the kind of pressure we're under?"

"No, but it can't be as hard as a battlefield."

"Can I have some water?"

"There's no room service down here."

"I'm in a basement?"

"Maybe, maybe not."

"So because your mother didn't get a glass of water, you're not going to give me any?"

"You can try and guess all you want what I'm going to do."

"I thought you were going to try to rape me."

"Did you?"

"At my house, I could feel it."

"Feel what?"

"You had an erection as you leaned against me. Is that what this is about?"

"An erection?" He laughed, then he reached inside his jacket and pulled a Beretta from his belt. "This is what you felt sticking into you, Pam. Is that what you want?"

She took a step backward and stumbled on a broken chair leg. She reached out to steady herself on the wall and broke a nail. He walked over to her, placed the muzzle against her forehead, and stared deeply into her cold eyes. He listened to Pam's rapid breathing in the silent room.

"You have to let me go," she said.

"Why?"

"I have a child."

"No, you don't. I've been checking up on you."

"How?"

"It ain't hard, and you ain't got no kids."

"I do."

"You don't, Pam. You'll stay here until you tell me all about it."

"About what?"

"All those things you've done."

"I don't know what you're talking about."

"Yes, you do."

"Is this about Dr. Truman again?"

"You tell me."

"How can I when I don't know what it is you're talking about?"

"You got into nursing because you like hurting the vulnerable."

"Look, I'm sorry about your mother."

"You will stay here, and each day it will increase, until you tell me."

"What is it you want me to confess to?"

"I think I'll start it now."

"Start what?"

"The film."

He pulled the gun away, tucked it into his belt, and turned his back. As he did, Pam picked up the chair leg and swung it at the back of his head, but he saw the shadow she cast beneath the bare bulb and dodged, then he threw her over his shoulder onto her back. Pam lay there winded as he opened the trunk. Then he lifted her up by her hair and threw her against the wall.

He pulled some rope out of the trunk, looping each end around his hands. He closed the trunk, forced her face down onto the floor, and tied her arms behind her back and her ankles together. There was a radiator in the room. He tied the end of the rope to it and turned Pam over so that she was sitting. Then he opened the door. Pam strained to see past him but it was dark outside. Some minutes later, he brought in a TV monitor with a DVD player. He set them on the floor and plugged them into the only wall socket.

"You're going to watch this film, and when I come back you're going to tell me all about it," he said.

"What is it, what are you making me watch?"

He used a remote control to turn the film on. The monitor, which sat directly opposite Pam, displayed the image of a wounded soldier. At first Pam wasn't sure if it was a fictional film or not. The images that followed left her in no doubt that this was real footage of horrific war injuries.

He watched the light from the screen flicker spectrally into the cold room. Then he hit the light switch, plunging Pam into a darkness lit only by the screen. She heard the door close and a bolt sliding into place as she closed her eyes, but the screams of the soldiers prevented her from sleeping.

She tried to watch, remembering his request that she tell him all about it. And as she did, she felt violated by the film and its tremendous insistence on injury too severe for medical aid. And her fear grew as she thought of the man, whose name she didn't even know, a man beyond reach, her jailer.

CHAPTER 39

Greg was woken early the next morning by the sound of his mobile ringing next to his ear. He reached out and answered without looking at the number.

"The price has gone up," the kidnapper said.

Greg sat up. "I haven't got the money, but we're trying to get it. This has all gotten out of hand. What are you doing to them?"

"Using the information you gave me."

"I didn't tell you to torture them and lock them in a glass cage."

"You said use their phobias to scare the other parties. What did you think? This was going to be a case of hire me and fire me? Two mill, that's what we agreed, but now I want four, and each day the price goes up. So if you want to see your daughter again, you better cough up, or I'm going to enjoy her, understand?"

"Enjoy her?"

"I think she's gagging for it."

"Look—"

The line went dead. He turned to see Felicity's angry face. She rose from the bed and stood in front of the mirror, brushing her hair.

They'd spent the night together and fragments of their lovemaking broke into Greg's mind like shards of glass. He remembered drinking a bottle of cheap supermarket brandy and her coming to him as he got ready for bed. She was naked, and the sight of her body aroused him too much for his own self-control, which was waning by the hour. The tension he'd felt since he revealed what he'd done was unbearable, and Felicity knew how to ease it. She always had, ever since the first time they'd made love. And as he looked at her toned figure and generous breasts, he thought of Julian again and his anger surfaced like a snake.

He was still trying to snatch back what had been stolen from him, and he could see his hands touching her in the dark, as if the physical contact could recall a broken past. But Julian had owned part of her all these years, and Greg felt as though he'd leased his wife and the little carnal pleasure she shared with him.

Or was it still an act? Did she want something more

dangerous from him? Felicity was dragging the brush roughly through her hair. Greg pictured her buttocks raw and bleeding, her body compliant to her submissive needs.

CHAPTER 40

When Micky Fallow turned up on Samantha's doorstep, she momentarily thought he was selling something. Then she looked at his clothes and the way he was standing with one hand against the door and she knew he was there to acquire. Julian's lies filled her head. She smelt cigar smoke and aftershave.

"Mrs. Villa?" he said.

"Yes, who are you?"

"My name is Fallow."

"Micky Fallow?"

"You know me?"

"I've heard mention of your name"

"I had some business interests tied up with your husband. Dreadful business what happened to him, I came to offer my condolences."

"And why is it I feel you've come to offer more than that?

"You're a perceptive woman, I can see, not just a pretty face. I like women like that."

"I don't know anything about my husband's affairs. I don't see how I can help you."

"Don't you?" he said.

He ran his eyes down her figure, pausing at her cleavage.

"All I know is Julian left a lot of debt," she said.

"I know, and I'm here to clear it."

"Oh really? And how are you going to do that?"

"I own his assets."

"He hasn't got any."

"There's this house, and its attractive contents."

"I own this house."

"You'll lose it to the bank, but I can write you a generous check that will see you clear."

"It sounds like I would be in your debt then."

"I'm sure you can find ways of paying me back."

CHAPTER 41

Pam lay in the dark. She heard no sound at all, not even distant traffic. She was hungry and raw. Her head was filled with images of wounded soldiers. The radiator was cold and hard against her back. As she wondered how long she'd been there, she heard the door open. A shaft of light spread across the room, and she looked up at Mary Wells's son.

"What you been up to Pam?" he said, closing the door.

Pam didn't say anything. She just stared at him as he came over with a knife. Then he slipped it under her legs and cut the rope that tethered her ankles together.

"Tell me about the film," he said.

"It's a film about war injuries."

"That all?"

"I need to eat something."

"You'll get food if you tell me what you felt as you looked at those men, brave men sent out to fight for the likes of you."

"I felt sick. It's appalling."

"You a nurse, and all."

"That didn't happen to you."

"No, it happened to someone I knew."

"Do you feel guilty?"

"What do you fucking think I feel?"

He pulled a knife from his belt and pressed its tip into the skin below her right eye. It was a Gerber infantry knife, and it left a tear drop of blood running down Pam's face.

CHAPTER 42

When Samantha slammed the door in Micky Fallow's face, he got back in his Bentley. He told Knuckles to wait while he made a few calls.

"Are you going to call in the debt?" Knuckles said.

"Of course I am. The lady just needs a little convincing."

"Muscle, Micky?"

"You don't use muscle on a woman like that, she'll see reason."

Micky called a few colleagues and asked what they knew of Julian's sex life. He was smiling when he got off the phone.

"Her old man liked a few hookers at his parties, the

ones he threw at his office, or should I say my office?"

"What are you gonna do?"

"Sell them."

"About her?" Knuckles said, nodding in the direction of the house.

"Use my natural charm. You see?" Micky said, leaning forward. "The thing about women like her is they know what their old man's up to and they don't care because they only want one thing, and that's money, so long as they get that, they'll spread their legs for their husbands and make the right noises, and why not me, old son?"

"Why not?"

"My lovely wife eats pies when she's alone. She thinks I don't know, but I know everything. I bought her tits. She's still a good shag. She knows I like the ladies. She pretends not to. I give her the things she wants, I know how they work, these women. So I reckon Samantha will take the check, meet me for lunch, and let me take her to a hotel somewhere. I bet she tastes nice."

"I bet she does."

"Better than a bloody pie."

"Filet mignon."

"Knuckles, hand me the check book."

Knuckles opened the glove compartment and removed a leather covered Coutts Bank check book. Fallow enjoyed the smell of the ink rising from the page as he purchased Samantha. He thought of her mouth, he thought of her breasts, and all the ways he would taste her. He felt aroused by just how expensive she was compared to Anne. And he wondered what Samantha sounded like when she groaned. Anne was a tart in bed, and that was all right. He liked tarts, they'd do anything for a price. He pictured depravity on Samantha's face as he opened the car door and walked up her path.

Samantha was in the bedroom, changing, when she heard the bell ring. She slipped into a violet skirt and matching blouse, then she stepped into a pair of black heels. She peered out of the bedroom window. She could see the Bentley parked a few houses away and a huge man in the driver's seat. She went downstairs and opened the door. Mick Fallow took a step toward her and handed her the check.

"There's half a mill there," he said.

Samantha glanced down at it. She was aware that her black bra was showing through the top of her blouse.

"I don't think so."

"Why not?"

"Because I don't trust you."

"It's a fair offer."

"This house is worth considerably more. What is this, a protection racket?"

"Now you've offended me, can I have glass of water?"

"No."

"A whiskey then."

"Get out of here before I call the police."

"Now you don't want to do that."

"Mr. Fallow, you're harassing me."

"There's more where that came from," he said, tapping the check.

Samantha began to close the door but he put his hand on it.

"Just what do you think you're doing?"

"I need to have a word with you."

He walked past her into the hall.

"Did I invite you in?" Samantha said.

"No, your husband did."

"Say what you have to say and leave."

"I can get you out of the debt he's left you in."

"And what do you want in return?"

"Like good food, do you?"

"What has that got to do with anything?"

"Meet me for lunch."

"Why would I meet you for lunch?"

"Because I know women like you."

"Do you?"

"I know what you need and I can give it you. Julian can't anymore."

"Take your money and get out of here."

"Come on, don't be like that."

"Right. I'm calling the police."

"Don't do that."

"Will you leave?"

"Nice bra," Fallow said and slipped the check into the top of it.

Samantha stepped away from him but Fallow kept walking toward her.

CHAPTER 45

Samantha had her back to the wall facing the front door as Micky Fallow grabbed her wrist and pushed his hand inside the cup of her bra. Then Samantha brought her knee up hard and Fallow bent down, groaning, still holding her by the wrist.

"So that's how you want to play it," he said.

She pulled away from him, but he tore her blouse open. As he touched her breasts, for a moment he thought she was going along with it, because she didn't fight. She was staring over his shoulder at the front door. Earl was running up the path and, as Fallow turned, Earl smashed him across the head with his motorbike helmet, knocking him to the floor. Fallow held his palm to the side of his face, saw the blood, and pulled a Luger from his pocket.

As he did, Earl stamped on his elbow. He lifted Mickey up by the collar and punched him in the face. Outside Knuckles stared at a woman bending over as she tended to her garden. His eyes traced the shape of her buttocks in her jeans. He didn't hear the commotion coming from the house where Fallow spat a tooth onto the tiles.

"Know who I am?" he said to Earl.

"Right now, you're my punching bag."

"You her bit on the side?"

"You better get out of here."

"I own this place and all she has."

"So you're Micky Fallow," Earl said.

"And who the fuck are you?"

"I'm looking for a man named Two Pence."

"Are you?"

"If you don't want me to rearrange your face, then tell me who he is."

CHAPTER 44

Micky Fallow didn't speak, so Earl hit him in the stomach. He delivered the blow with such ferocity that Fallow's feet left the floor. Then Earl brought his knee up into his face. Earl hit him again, knocking him over, and Fallow held his hands up.

"You should work for me, son," he said.

"And why would I want to do that?"

"I need fellas hurt sometimes."

"Are you going to tell me who he is?"

"Never heard of him."

"You're lying."

"Dear oh dear, what makes you think I know this bloke?"

"Greg Sheen asked you if you knew any burglars and you suggested him."

"Did I?"

"I haven't even begun to hurt you."

Earl picked up the Luger and pressed it against Fallow's head.

"All right," Fallow said.

Earl stepped back as Fallow got to his feet. He removed a bright white cotton handkerchief from his pocket and dabbed at his face. His lip was smashed and bleeding heavily.

"Are you going to tell me?" Earl said.

"Two Pence is a fella called Spencer, but he don't use that name, he uses his middle name, Leonard, his name's Leonard Wells, and you do not want to cross him."

"Where can I find him?"

"Beats me."

"You need to do better than that."

"Honest, I don't know. He left the army some years ago, used to live with his mother in Kew. He ain't there now. Leonard's always been a time bomb."

"Do you have a contact number for him?"

"I might do."

"That your goon out there?"

"He works for me."

"You give me the number and address you have for him, and you walk away. You get him to drive you out of here, understood?"

CHAPTER 45

Francis Truman woke early the next morning. He got up, donned his bright canary yellow dressing gown, and left the bedroom in search of coffee. As he walked into the kitchen, he saw a shape behind the door. He turned to see Mary Wells's son standing there in army fatigues and leather gloves. The man reached out and grabbed him by the neck.

"You, from the hospital," Truman said in a choked voice.

"That's right, and I have a surprise date for you, Francis." Mr. Wells lifted him off the floor. "You ready for her, are you, Franky boy?"

"What are you talking about?"

But the man didn't answer. He just smiled and reached into his pocket.

When Truman came to, he thought he'd been given

an anaesthetic. The first thing he felt was a sense of unde-
fined outrage. His mind searched for a credible explana-
tion of what it was he was angry about. Some deed that
simply did not happen to an eminent surgeon had been
perpetrated against his person, but his thoughts were like
cotton wool and drifted away from him, as his eyes adjusted to the darkness. Then he recalled the scene in the
kitchen, and he realised the lunatic who'd assaulted two
guards had broken into his house and put chloroform over
his mouth.

Truman raised his head and heard someone breathing
next to him. He reached out a hand and felt a leg. A
woman gasped a few inches from his head. He tried to
stand, reaching out to steady himself on the cold floor.
Then the door opened and Mr. Wells walked in, turning
the light on.

"Ain't you two a pair?" he said.

Truman could see Pam tied up, rope encircling her
wrists and legs.

"Now listen here. You're going to release us," Truman said.

"Am I?"

"You are."

"Maybe I will, if you do something for me."

"What?"

"I want you to operate on Pam."

"Are you mad?"

"How would you treat dehydration?

"You need psychiatric help."

"That's what they say in the army, the posh twats who send off others to fight."

"Do you know what they'll give you when they catch you?"

"Dose of clap?"

"Now you listen to me."

"No, you listen to me."

Mr. Wells pulled the Gerber from his belt and held the tip of the knife against Truman's cheek.

"Do you think I'm going to perform an illegal operation?" Truman said.

"I'll find your limit, and then you'll see the kind of man you are."

"Has he hurt you?" Truman said to Pam.

"I need some water."

"Do you hear that, Doc? She's thirsty."

"Well, give her something to drink."

"You get it."

"How?"

"Find a tap."

"All right, are you going to let me through that door?"

"I'm going to give you some time to think it over," Leonard said.

"My wife will have returned. She'll have called the police."

"When I come back, I want to watch you do it to her."

"Do what?"

"What do you think?"

Mr. Wells ran the knife down Truman's cheek, giving him a two inch gash that dripped blood onto the concrete floor. Then he left them alone in the darkness.

CHAPTER 48

The door closed, and they heard the bolt sliding into place.

"Are you hurt, Pam?" Truman said.

"Slightly cut, more scared than anything."

"Do you know where we are?"

"No idea. I've listened and listened, but you can't hear anything. I think we're underground."

"There has to be a way out."

"I think he's planning to kill us."

"I'll have to tackle him."

"Have you seen how strong he is?"

"I could hit him where it hurts."

"I don't think it's going to be that easy."

"We can't let him get away with this."

"I don't know what's worse, giving him what he wants or not."

"Have you seen any other parts of the building?"

"Only the corridor outside. When he first brought me here there was a trunk in this room. Then he took it outside. You can just see it in the corridor when he opens the door. I can't remember anything between my flat and being here. I don't even know which part of London we're in."

"That will be the chloroform. He used it on me too. I have no recall of anything after he attacked me in my kitchen."

CHAPTER 47

Micky Fallow was halfway through a bottle of single malt when he wondered where Anne was. He'd been stitched up by his private doctor and had his missing tooth seen to by his dentist after Earl had beaten him up. Fallow had made a few phone calls to find out who Earl was, then spent the evening with Anne. She'd cheered him up, put on a performance for him, taking it slow in the living room, the way she used to, dancing in her bra and G-string, teasing him, glancing at his crotch. Fallow sat in the leather chair he favored for the sex shows Anne and other ladies put on for him. She threw her bra at him and swung her tits in two clean circles then turned, bent, and slipped the G-string off, giving him a good glimpse between her thighs.

He'd taken her upstairs and done it in the bedroom, feeling slightly too married but too drunk to care. Entering Anne after she dimmed the lights, he thought of Samantha and realized that Anne still had it. Now, as he sat there, sipping the malt, he looked at his watch. It was eleven a.m. He'd woken up late and found her gone. She was probably shopping. He got up and looked at his face in the mirror. He was going to get Earl Blake.

༺ೋೋ༻

As Fallow picked up the phone to call Knuckles, Anne was entertaining a friend. She was astride a large man with a chest so hairy it looked like a carpet. She raised and lowered herself on her haunches, guiding his cock in and out of her until he groaned. Then she climbed off the bed.

"You enjoy that, Jimmy?"

"Oh, yeah, you got what it takes, Anne."

"And so do you, big boy. I'm gonna take a shower."

"Then I got something for you."

She went into the bathroom, closed the door and stood under the hot water, rubbing soap into her breasts, fingering herself until she achieved the orgasm men rarely gave her, certainly not her husband.

She thought of Jimmy's hirsute skin and shuddered. She admired her body in the mirror as she toweled herself down.

Then she went into the bedroom, naked, relaxed, and watched as Jimmy lumbered about the room, his dick drooping beneath his enormous body.

"I thought you'd like this," he said, handing her a black box.

Anne opened it, then opened her eyes wide. "Jimmy, you shouldn't have."

"They're the best diamonds around."

"I can see that. I've got a favor to ask, just a little one."

She slid the ring on her finger, held it up to the light, lowered her eyes, and took Jimmy in her hand.

Jimmy was a good listener. The ring suited Anne.

He held the door open for her as they left the hotel they used in central London, Jimmy getting a good look at Anne's arse in the tight skirt she was wearing. Then the man, known as Jimmy Peach to the gangland world, watched Anne drive away in the Mercedes E-Class Cabriolet Micky Fallow had bought her and liked to see her drive naked on his estate.

Jimmy was known as the peach because that is what he called pussy. He'd been seeing Anne for a few months now. As he walked to his Rolls-Royce, he thought about what she'd asked him to do.

⁊ↄ⁊ↄ

Earl visited the flat where Leonard had lived with his

mother. The contact number Micky Fallow had given him was out of use. It was the same number Greg had for Leonard before he got rid of his mobile. Earl spoke to the estate agents responsible for letting the flat and got the same information they gave to the police.

He found the army records for Spencer Wells. He also found out that he had a brother, Harry, and obtained his address from a contact. Two days after he beat Fallow up, on a wet Saturday afternoon, Earl drove to Harry's house and parked in a disused drive some yards away. He'd hired a van and sat there with a sandwich, a coffee, and a pair of binoculars.

Fallow had given him a good description of Leonard. Earl had bought a mobile phone with cash, and posted a note to Harry that read:

"We need to speak to your brother Leonard, business for him, call this number."

Now he waited as the rain washed the street, knowing he might be in for a week's stint sitting around. That Saturday he saw only Mandy leaving then returning with some shopping a few hours later. As he was about to leave for the day his mobile rang. He recognised the voice as Leonard's from the time Greg had spoken to him.

"Who is this?" Leonard said.

"Friend of Micky's."

"Micky Fallow?"

"Yeah, that's right."

"What do you want?"

"Got a job for you."

"What kind of job?"

"Simple break-in."

"Whereabouts?"

"Office in South London."

"What do you want taken?"

"Some documents."

"It'll cost you a thousand."

"Good. Where can I meet you?"

There was a pause. "The Willoughby Arms in King-ston."

"When?"

"Monday evening, seven o'clock."

"Okay."

"Bring the money. What do you look like?"

"Six two, dark hair. And you?"

"No need to worry about that, I'll find you."

The line went dead.

Earl switched off his mobile and drove away. Later that evening he went round to see Samantha. They sat in the living room and drank wine. He told her about the meeting.

"What do you plan to do? He'll recognise you," she said.

"I won't be in the pub when he arrives. I've been to it. There are two entrances, one at the front and a side entrance by the gents'. There's an alley nearby, from where you can see both entrances. I'll wait. When he leaves, I'll tackle him. This time he won't get a chance to fight back. I'll slip him the blackjack and knock him out. I'll hold him until he gives up the address where he's keeping Michael and Abby."

Samantha sipped her drink.

"That man's been back, sniffing around."

"Micky Fallow?"

"He rang the bell earlier, I didn't answer. He had that ogre with him."

"I'll take care of him."

"How about me, Earl? Now that I'm a single woman again, will you take care of me?"

They went into the bedroom. Earl peeled her dress from her and entered her hungry body on the silk sheets.

CHAPTER 48

Francis Truman was hungry and cold. He rested against Pam, who was shivering in the dark as the bolt slid open and Mr. Wells walked in.

"Cosy, nice," he said.

Truman raised his head wearily. "We're trying to keep warm."

"Of course, you are."

"We need food."

"You know what to do if you want that."

"You're treating us like animals."

"Just like the way you treat your patients, isn't it?"

"No, it is not," Truman said. "I'm a surgeon, and Pam is an excellent nurse."

"What are you going to do to us?" Pam said.

"Let you go if you and the doc here do what I tell you."

"You can't be serious," Truman said.

"Do I look like I'm joking?"

"I'm not going to perform an operation on her."

"You fancy her, don't you?"

"That again?"

"I'll bring you some food now. Pam, you can have a glass of water. I want you to be strong enough for what happens next."

"And what does happen next?" she said.

"Don't worry, if you and the doc want to have a quick shag go ahead."

"Where are we?" Truman said.

"You're at my gaff, Francis."

As they waited for him to return, Truman could hear Pam breathing beside him. He thought about the times he'd desired her on the ward. He reached out and touched her leg. He felt aroused and was faced with a reality whose moral circumstances challenged the basic things he believed about himself, that he was a good man, whose professionalism placed him a cut above others and who never took advantage of anyone else.

The door opened again and Mr. Wells came in with two plates. They could smell chicken.

"Tuck in," he said.

"What then?" Truman said.

"You go to the cinema."

"What?"

Mr. Wells cut the ropes from Pam's wrists and legs. She rubbed the circulation back into them and got to her feet. They ate with their hands. Mr. Wells watched them for a while then left the room.

"What's he talking about?" Truman said.

"He's going to play us a film of wounded soldiers."

CHAPTER 49

Abby's hunger pains were getting worse. She kept drinking from the tiny sink in the toilet. She'd been trying to calculate how long it was since they'd seen their kidnapper, the man she loathed and feared but whom she depended on for food, and she realised it was impossible to tell the time in the glass house, as if there was only one reality there, and it was a constant of pain and fear. Michael sat with his face against the wall. His body was slumped, and she couldn't see his face. She'd been trying to get his attention and now she raised her voice.

"Michael, you haven't moved for hours," she said.

He got up and walked to the front of his cage. "I need to eat something," he said.

"He's got to have the money by now."

"I thought I heard a scraping sound, like when he comes through the ceiling."

"It's been days since he's come down here."

"Maybe he's just left us."

"What if something's happened to him?" Abby said.

"No one would find us."

"He's the only person who knows where we are."

"We've got to make a fight for it," Michael said.

"We're too weak."

"After I've eaten, the next time he comes in, I'll jump him."

"I think I can hear him."

They stared up at the ceiling but it didn't open.

CHAPTER 50

That Monday morning as Abby and Michael talked, Leonard was in bed with Mandy. He'd gone to visit his mother and told her his new house would be ready soon. He'd shown her an estate agent printout of a house worth over a million and been looked at with the blank gaze of incredulity. But Greg was going to pay him and, when Leonard had the money, he'd show them, especially Harry.

As he was leaving, Mandy kissed him on the mouth. She ran her hands down his chest and opened his fly. And Leonard thought he'd enjoy her again, just once more, before he became a millionaire. So they went into the spare room. And as Mandy stripped, Leonard knew that his life before the army was permanently lost to him.

He'd known the kind of pleasure Mandy offered when he was younger. But now it was like trying to conjure a memory out of sand. She stood there watching him, naked, with that old expression on her face, a look halfway between provocation and desire. And a series of images stuttered through his mind, snapshots of the past—of Mandy and him making love in the back of his van and of her face beneath him as she came. He looked at her breasts and kissed her nipples. He touched her between her legs and felt pleasure in deceiving Harry, who'd taken her away, and all she might have offered him.

What future they might have had was spent that Monday morning in the heated exchange of lust and liquid on the spare bed. And it was different this time. Mandy seemed hungrier, more aroused, and Leonard held back, giving her one orgasm after another as he thought of the two posh kids in the glass house. Then he thought of Pam and what he would do to her and he released his clenched orgasm like a sexual punch. Mandy felt his pleasure swell inside her like a rose.

They lay there and Leonard tried to feign tenderness, but it was gone, and he knew his heart was untenanted by the softness a woman needs.

"What is it, Len?" Mandy said.

"You're Harry's."

"I'm yours, too, if you want me. I always loved the sex with you."

"But your Harry's property now."

"I ain't no one's property."

"I got to go," Leonard said, standing up.

"What's up with you, Len?"

"It all changed in the war."

"You talking about Kenny."

"Yes, and seeing how England works."

"What does that mean?"

"Class, Mandy. The likes of me get used, we just get fucked over."

"It ain't like the old days. You and Harry come from the same background, and Harry's done okay."

"This ain't just about money, Mandy. It's about the fact that the toffs can get away with things, while some-one like Kenny gets put in the line of fire."

"At least you came back uninjured."

"You know soldiers carry it all, and the MOD don't give them no compensation," he said, referring to those bastards in the Ministry of Defense. "We're badly paid lumps of meat that end up on the butcher's block."

"Len, you could still get a job, you could do a lot with your life."

"Doing what?"

"You could work for Harry, you were a good plumb-er."

"Come on, Mandy."

"We could see each other more."

"I'm about to make a lot of money."

"How?"

Just then the door opened and Harry walked in. "I thought I heard voices," he said. "I came back for some tools and find you fucking my brother."

He said it to Mandy, ignoring Leonard completely. Mandy got up from the bed and began dressing hurriedly. Harry watched her for a few seconds, glanced at Leonard, then walked over to Mandy and took hold of her arms. There was a frozen moment when they just looked at each other, all the pleasure that had been there on Mandy's face a few minutes before washed away by the guilt she was now feeling, and which Leonard knew too well.

Harry looked into her eyes with an expression that was unreadable. Then he hit her. He slapped her across the cheek, turning her face toward Leonard, who was standing watching them, feeling like the outsider.

Then Leonard moved toward him. He punched Harry so hard he knocked him onto the bed.

"She ain't your property," Leonard said.

And as Leonard raised his fist to hit Harry again, Mandy grabbed his arm. "Stop."

Leonard took his clothes and dressed in the hall.

Mandy pulled the rest of her clothes on as Harry got up, went into the kitchen, and applied paper towels to his bleeding nose. She came out into the hall as Leonard was opening the door. "Len, stay, we all need to talk."

"I ain't part of this, Mandy. I'm all on my own."

She watched him walk away down the gravel drive, his posture erect, his strides like a military march. Then she went into the kitchen and looked at Harry's face as he began to sob.

CHAPTER 51

The second film was worse. After Pam and Truman had eaten the chicken and drunk the water Mr. Wells left for them, he came in and tied them both up at knifepoint. Then he set the monitor in front of them and left them with the images that populated his head. They stared at the reel of horror and tried to sleep, but the volume was too high. Eventually the film ended, and they were left with only the blank screen.

It was midday when Leonard returned. After he left Harry's, he'd gone to his room and worked out with weights, not noticing his brother's blood on his knuckles, seeing only the glass house and his prisoners as he bench-pressed his muscles relentlessly into iron.

He had his army uniform on as he untied Truman

and got him to his feet. "Answer right and you go," he said.

"You do know the prison sentence this carries?"

"Do you think I'm afraid of prison?"

"I understand how you feel about your mother, but we take great care to look after our patients."

"First question, have you shagged Pam?"

"No."

"Do you want to?"

"This is absurd."

"Do you want to?"

"Pam is an attractive woman, but we have a professional relationship."

"You've got a choice, you either admit to medical malpractice, or I will hurt one of you. It may be Pam. Are you willing to risk that?"

"You want me to admit to something I haven't done?"

"You have."

"And what malpractice am I guilty of?"

"You allowed my mother to get hypothermia then lied about it."

"Do you realise how many patients we have, what hours we do?"

"I don't give a fuck about your hours." Leonard drew the Gerber and placed it just below Truman's lips. "Lie to me and I'll cut your fucking tongue out," he said.

Truman looked at the blood on his knuckles. "I

wasn't at the hospital when this happened," he said.

"You were, Pam, weren't you?"

"Yes, but I didn't see it."

"Because you don't give a shit."

"That's not true. Why do you think I became a nurse?"

"Because you wanted to shag a doctor."

"Were you treated for your psychological injuries?" Truman said.

"What do you think?" Leonard said.

Then he sliced Truman's lower lip in two. It tore like tomato skin, shedding blood onto the doctor's shirt. Leonard grabbed him by the hair and dragged him over to Pam. He pushed Truman's head into her face and smeared his blood all over her cheeks, then he slapped her to stop her from screaming as he cut her ropes and pulled her to her feet.

Truman was getting up when Leonard kicked him in the ribs. "You stay down on the floor if I fucking tell you to," he said. He held the knife to Pam's right eye, the tip touching her lashes, a millimetre from her eyeball. "I've killed with this knife," Leonard said.

"If you kill us, they'll catch you. Don't worsen your situation," Truman said.

"Either you do as I say or Pam loses an eye."

"I admit we got things wrong with your mother," Truman said.

"Fucking right. It wasn't too smart calling them guards. See what I did to them?"

"I heard."

"Does it matter to you if I blind Pam?"

"Of course."

"Show me how much."

"How?"

"Pam, if I remove the Gerber and hurt him, really hurt him, do you care?"

"Yes, I'm a nurse."

"I know you are, but you're something else as well."

"What?"

Leonard grinned and put the knife away. He went out into the hall and returned with a nurse's uniform.

"Put it on," he said, throwing it at Pam. "You're going to show us what you are."

"Here?"

"Our changing rooms are being decorated."

"Then what?"

"You'll see."

Pam began to put it on over her clothes but Leonard stopped her. "Properly, don't be shy."

She turned her back and removed her skirt and blouse, then put it on.

"Now see to the doctor."

"See to him?"

"His lip's cut."

"I haven't got any equipment. He needs stitches."

"Kiss it better."

He took her by the back of her neck and forced her lips to Truman's. He held her there, locked in a grotesque embrace and when he let go Pam wiped the back of her hand across her mouth.

"Does he disgust you, wiping it away like that?" Leonard said.

"My hand's smeared with blood. Why do you think I did it?"

"If I leave you with your eyes, I will leave you with things you will never stop seeing."

"Do you have a first aid kit?"

Leonard reached into his pocket and removed a needle and cotton. He handed it to Pam. "Stitch him up, Pam."

"This needle's dirty."

"So are you, you can do it naked."

"Have you got a lighter?"

"Take your clothes off."

"Alcohol then?"

"If you don't stitch his lip, I'll cut the other one in half, then yours."

"I'll get an infection," Truman said.

"It's that, or I'll make sure you get hypothermia."

Pam went over to Truman and inspected his lip.

"It's not as bad as it looks," she said.

"If you don't stitch it, then you dance naked," Leonard said. "Do it properly and I'll let you go."

Pam removed the nurse's uniform, then her bra and panties, shivering, her eyes focused on the wall. Then she raised her hands and swayed her hips.

CHAPTER 52

Leonard picked Truman's head up and forced him to watch Pam dance. His mouth looked like a red smear on his pale face as he stared at his nurse, naked, grotesque in her performance. Leonard looked for arousal in the doctor's face and saw a glimmer of something he was repressing.

Leonard turned to Pam and looked at the way she was moving. "Make it more sexual."

"Like this?" she asked, swaying from side to side.

"If you turn him on, you get to go."

"You mean that?"

"You have to make it sexy, show him you want him."

"And what about him?"

"Watch her do it, Doc, want her."

Pam moved toward Truman and stared down at him as he gazed up at her. His eyes tried to tell a different story—a story of denial, of morality, and professionalism—but she searched for something else there, the thing he wouldn't admit to himself and which she knew he felt. She'd seen it in the way he talked to her. She'd caught him looking at her, and the day she decided to get Mr. Wells thrown out of the hospital, she'd known how Truman would react.

And now Pam seduced Truman in front of their captor, feeling part of a porn show. She parted her legs and touched her body, measuring his eyes for desire. She caressed her breasts, moving the way she'd seen them move at the strip club she'd gone to once as a student. It wasn't real, Pam told herself. She was following their captor's orders to save their lives. She was putting on a show, using her body to fool their abductor in the bare room.

Truman began to want Pam and entered into a moral conflict with himself and the person he thought he was.

Leonard saw it between them, and he watched with pleasure as they unmasked their sexual desires.

Pam danced and Truman watched, his gaze locked on her body with an expression that bordered between hatred and lust.

Then Leonard put his hand on Pam's shoulder. "Touch him," he said.

CHAPTER 55

The things Leonard wanted to do to Pam were must have shown in his eyes, because she looked away from him as he stared at his secret film. It had been running in his head since he had sex with Mandy. And now he wanted to make Pam part of it.

She sensed the danger if she didn't comply and thought of release, turning to her colleague, a man for whom she harboured desire, lost in the unreal performance.

Pam reached down and put her hand between the doctor's legs. She tried to look at him with pity, a recognition of their mutual humiliation, and then she realised she was insulting him, and that she had to feign it completely or they would die. But Truman was hard and Pam felt relieved. She laid his hands on her breasts then pulled away, knowing the acts she'd performed had fractured any lasting chance of romance with him in the outside world. She wanted to cheapen and demean their kidnapper.

"Let us go now," she said to Mr. Wells.

"Do you want to shag her?" he said to Truman.

"Haven't you pushed this far enough?"

"Answer the question and you leave."

"How do we know you're telling the truth?"

"Do you want Pam?"

"Yes."

"Pam, do you want him?"

"He's a handsome man."

"So you'd let him screw you?"

"Yes, but not here."

"Did you mistreat my mother?"

"We did."

"What do you think about it now?" he said, looking at Truman.

"I can see we were negligent. I will see it doesn't happen again."

"I'll get you some water, then you can leave."

Pam got dressed as he left the room. He returned with two glasses of water and watched them drink them.

"Would you see to someone who needed medical attention?" he said.

"Of course," Truman said.

"You're true pros, ain't you?"

"You said you'd let us go."

"That's what I'm doing."

"So you'll let us walk out here?" Pam said.

"That's right."

"Dr. Truman?" Pam said.

She reached out her hand and helped him to his feet, feeling disingenuous in her formality. Leonard stepped aside and they went out into the corridor.

There was staircase at the end and they went up it and stood facing a door. Truman tried the handle but it was locked. Pam saw they were standing on what looked like a trap door. They moved to one side and opened it. They stepped onto the ladder at its top. And Pam and Truman descended it, tasting freedom. They descended all the way into the glass house.

CHAPTER 54

As they stepped off the ladder, Pam and Truman stared at the glass cages. Abby and Michael pressed their faces to the glass.

"What is this place?" Truman said.

"This is the glass house," Michael said.

Then their captor came down wearing his hood.

"You said you'd let us go," Pam said.

"Welcome to the glass house."

"How many people are you keeping prisoner?" Truman said.

"It will be one less in a moment."

He pulled the Gerber from his belt and slashed Truman's throat. Blood sprayed Pam's face.

Her screams were nothing compared to those of Abby, who began to bash her head against the glass. "He's going to kill us, I told you, Michael," she said.

The man slapped Pam's face.

"Did you really think I was going to let you go?"

"What are you doing to these people?"

"Handing them a vanity mirror, one I stole from your purse."

"I did what you asked."

"Women like you always do." He walked over to Michael's cage. "You want to get out?"

"Of course, we do."

"Then you're going to have to lock Abby in with her snakes."

"I'm not doing that."

"It's either that, or Abby leaves you with the spiders."

"No, not after what we've been through," she said.

He left them alone in the dark and the cold.

CHAPTER 55

It was two p.m. when Earl saw Micky Fallow lurking in the garden with Knuckles by his side. Earl caught the glint of knuckleduster on Knuckles's huge hand as he came round the side of the property. He'd been expecting them. Samantha had called him, saying she'd seen the Bentley parked outside, and Earl figured Fallow would return to take what he saw as his. Now Earl moved silently across the lawn, coming up behind them, gripping his blackjack in his clenched fist. They were standing at the back of the house as he gained on them.

Fallow turned as he heard him approach, then Earl cracked the blackjack across Knuckles's skull. Knuckles fell to the ground like a sack of bricks. Fallow swung at Earl. He ducked, came up in a blur, and swung a right

hook at Fallow's jaw that sent him crashing against a
wall. Earl looked down at Knuckles, who was out. He
moved in on Fallow as he pulled his Luger from the
pocket of his cashmere coat. He was raising it as Earl
kicked his forearm, knocking the gun loose from his grip.

"Do you know how many Lugers I own?" Fallow
said. "You've still got one of them."

"Well, you're not having it," Earl said, "and you're
not having Samantha."

Earl punched him square on the nose, breaking it. He
knocked him to the ground and continued hitting him until Fallow lay there without moving.

He got a wheelbarrow from the shed and carted
Knuckles to the Bentley. He did the same with Fallow,
locking them in the car. Then he went inside the house,
where Samantha was waiting for him in the living room.

"They won't be troubling you again," he said.

"You don't think he'll be back?"

"I locked them in their car. They're out cold. I just
called the police and reported two men acting suspicious-
ly in a Bentley. They'll find the gun on him."

Later, he noticed the flashing lights outside. From
the living room window, he saw Fallow and Knuckles
taken away in an ambulance, a police car following.

Earl made love to Samantha in the twilight, and her
skin looked silver in the thin strip of moonlight that shone
through the window. Then he got ready to meet Leonard
Wells.

CHAPTER 56

L eonard put on the hood and went down into the glass house. Pam was sitting with her back to a wall when he stepped off the ladder. Leonard walked over to her and pulled her to her feet. Then he pointed at Abby's cage.

"There's a door back there," he said. "You can leave now, Pam."

"The only way out of here is through the ceiling," Pam said.

"Let me show you. Abby and Michael would like to watch this, they like people in masks."

He guided her to the back of Abby's cage, holding her by the shoulders. He stood behind the plywood panelling that formed the toilet.

"You said there was a door here," Pam said.

"There is."

Leonard tore her blouse from her, forcing her to the ground. Pam kicked and screamed as Abby looked away and Michael gazed at the wall.

Leonard pulled off Pam's skirt, her bra, and panties as she tried to push him off.

"Shame about the doc," he said.

"I'd never fuck a man like you," Pam said.

"Too common for you, am I?"

"You're disgusting."

She spat at him. Leonard stood and wiped the saliva from his cheek as she got to her feet.

"I don't fancy you, Pam," Leonard said.

He grabbed her by the throat with his left hand and pushed her against the wall. He drew the Gerber from his belt. Then, reaching down between her legs, he rammed the blade inside her, all the way past its serrated edge, to the hilt. "I wouldn't shag a tart like you."

Pam put her hand to her ruined genitals and stared at the blood, her body like a wound in the glass wall of Abby's cage, her face spectral in its reflection. Leonard grabbed her by her hair and pulled her head back so that the skin on her neck was tight. Then he sliced her throat and dragged her to the front of the cages.

"I'll come back for you, Abby," he said. "I reckon you're worth a shag."

He removed his hood and Abby and Michael stared

at his face. Then Leonard climbed up the ladder and got ready to meet Mickey's friend, his new client.

It was seven p.m. when he left. Two teenagers were loitering near his dirt bike, and Leonard glared at them until they walked away. Then he kick-started it and rode to Kingston beneath a moonlit sky.

CHAPTER 57

Earl had arrived at the pub early. He checked inside, to see if Leonard was there, then took up his position in the alley from where he could see the front entrance.

At seven-thirty p.m. he sighted Leonard. He walked swiftly to the pub, going in through the front door. Earl waited. After twenty-five minutes he saw Leonard leave.

Earl bent over, clutching his stomach, then he called out Leonard's name. Leonard stopped and looked around.

A man was standing back from the mouth of the alley, and Leonard couldn't see his face but he could make out someone was there.

"I was meant to be meeting you," the man said, "but I've been attacked, stabbed. I need your help."

"You brought the money?" Leonard said and walked over to him, his hand on the knife in his pocket.

As Leonard got to the alley, the man's face came into focus and there was a moment when he registered recognition. Then Earl swung the blackjack at him.

He hit Leonard in the forehead, opening it up and knocking him backward. Leonard pulled his knife, but Earl struck him across the arm, knocking the weapon to the ground. Leonard put his arm up to block Earl's next blow, but Earl hit him in the temple, knocking him out cold.

He dragged Leonard through the alley to the deserted street at the back where he'd parked the van. He bundled him into the back, tied his legs and arms with duct tape, and gagged him.

CHAPTER 58

When Leonard regained consciousness, he saw a flash of trees then the light outside darkened.

Earl pulled into a garage he owned in Hammersmith. He locked the door, turned on the single light bulb that dangled from a rust-colored wire, and opened the back of the van.

Earl was wearing a pair of shooting gloves and holding Micky Fallow's Luger. He pointed it at Leonard's head and motioned to the tape around his legs. "Now I'm going to cut that off. If you try anything, you get a bullet in both legs. When I cut the tape, you'll get up and walk to that chair," he said, pointing with his other hand to a small wooden chair at the far end of the garage next to a work bench. "Then you're going to give up the location where you're holding Michael Villa and Abby Sheen. I'll leave you here while I go to find them. If you mess with me, I'll hurt you, understand? Nod your head for yes, Leonard."

Leonard met his eyes with defiance and rage. There was a pause after Earl finished speaking, then Leonard nodded.

Earl walked over to the bench at the back of the garage and got a knife. Then he climbed into the van, the Luger aimed at Leonard's knees, as he slashed the duct tape.

Earl climbed out while keeping the gun trained on Leonard. "Get out."

Leonard got to his feet and jumped out into the garage. Then he walked over to the chair and sat down.

"Okay, I'm going to take the gag off, and we're going to talk," Earl said.

He waited until Leonard nodded then he pulled the tape off roughly.

"Where are you keeping them?"

"I don't know who you're talking about."

Earl smashed him across the jaw with the butt of the Luger, knocking his head sideways. Leonard sprayed the wall with blood and saliva.

"Think again," Earl said.

"If I knew, I'd tell you. What makes you think I know these people?"

"Because Greg Sheen hired you to kidnap them,. I know all about it. He's made a full confession. He's remorseful now and wants his daughter back. Once again, where are they?"

"I told you, I don't know nothing about it."

Earl went behind Leonard and got a two inch nail and a hammer. "You've still got time to reconsider," Earl said. "No? Okay then. Let me explain. This is not a long nail but it will hurt. The next one will go in deeper, understand?"

Leonard kept his eyes on him but said nothing.

Earl positioned the point on his right knee cap and drove it in hard with the hammer. Leonard bit his lip to avoid screaming, but a small groan of pain escaped from his mouth.

"Where are they, Leonard? You could avoid a lot of hurt here."

"I ain't never heard of no Michael and Abby."

"You're lying."

"I ain't."

"I think you're angry you haven't got the money, but it isn't there."

"What money?"

"The two million you were going to split with Greg. I saw you at the warehouse. It's no use trying to dodge this one."

"Do what you have to do. Are you gonna pop me?"

"If I have to."

"I don't think you got it in you."

"Don't you?"

"You ain't a killer. I reckon it took all you got to drive that nail in."

"I've killed before."

"You ex-army?"

Earl nodded.

"You wouldn't want to do time," Leonard said.

"Who says I'd do time? This is Micky Fallow's gun and his prints are all over it."

Earl got a flamethrower from the wall and fired it up.

"All right," Leonard said. "I'll tell you."

"There's a good boy."

Earl turned the heat off. "I do like cooperation."

"I've got them, but I still want paying."

"The money's not there. Greg believed that Michael's father would pay, and Michael's father is not only bankrupt, he's dead, thanks to Fallow."

"I ain't telling you if I don't get paid. That Greg's like all the other stuck-up fuckers who let you down."

"There isn't any money. What do you think this is? I kidnap you and pay you? No, you tell me where they are, and I keep you here until I make sure they're okay."

There was a moment when Leonard looked away, past Earl, at the bare walls of the garage. But he wasn't looking at the walls, he was seeing Kenny's face, and remembering the man he used to be.

"They're at the glass house."

"I've seen the films, where is it?"

"My gaff."

"And where is that?"

"It's a garage. They're in the basement. You get to it through a trapdoor."

CHAPTER 59

Leonard gave him the address and told him the key was in his pocket. Earl tied him to the chair, gagged him with duct tape, and fished the key out. Then he gunned the van all the way there.

The garage was located at the rear of some council flats in Kew. There were a few other garages, most of them disused. One had a broken door. Through the gap Earl could see piles of rotting cardboard boxes. Leonard's garage was the last one, an innocuous-looking façade that housed the torture cages. The whole area smelled of neglect and weeds. Broken bottles adorned the crumbling wall at the end. Used condoms lay among the debris thrown there by teenagers looking for a place to get a fix, either narcotic or sexual. The last garage had a lock on it.

The key fitted. Earl opened the door and walked in slowly. He found the light switch and took in the bare room, the single bed, magazines, weights, and cupboard. He went into the bathroom, a tiny confined space with a walk-in shower, a toilet, and sink. Behind the shower was another, smaller door.

He tried the handle and found it was locked. He looked for a key on the ledge and in the bathroom cabinet. Leonard had told him that the trapdoor lay beyond the bathroom. He hadn't said the door was locked, nor how to open it. Earl raised his leg and kicked it in. The wood splintered, and he created a hole large enough to walk through. Then he was in the hall, a cramped space about two foot square with a staircase leading down to a room and a trapdoor in the floor. Earl pulled it open. He saw a dark room below him and felt the cold rushing up from it. He lowered the ladder and heard it touch the ground. Then he climbed down.

As he took the first step he noticed a light switch on the ceiling. He flicked it and stared down at the glass house.

Then he climbed down and stood there facing the cages. And beyond them he saw the carnage Leonard had left Abby and Michael with. He looked at the bodies of a man and a woman. Blood had pooled across the floor and dried on the fronts of the glass cages.

"It's all right, I've come to get you out of here," he said.

"He killed them. Where is he?" Michael said.

"Don't worry, I've got him."

Abby started crying. "Who are you?"

"Earl Blake. Michael's mother hired me to find you. Is there anyone else you've seen while you've been here?"

"Just them. He's been torturing us. Who is he?"

"His name's Leonard Wells."

"There's a way of opening the roof," Michael said, "that's how he gets into the cages."

Earl climbed up the ladder and got on top of Abby's. There was a lock and once again he had no key.

"Go to the back and hold your hands over your ears," he said.

He waited until she was far enough away, then he blew the lock off with the Luger. He opened the roof and lay flat on the cage, then he reached his arm down. "Abby, grab my hand and I'll pull you up."

She could just reach it. Earl gripped her hand tightly, lifted her to the roof, and pulled her out. Abby climbed down the ladder as Earl blew the lock on Michael's cage and pulled him out. He noticed they were shivering.

"Do you need medical attention?"

"No," Abby said.

"I just want to go home," Michael said.

"Let's get out of here."

They climbed the ladder. Earl went first, to check that there was no one up there, then Abby went up, followed by Michael. They both stared at the room occupied by their kidnapper, and then they were outside. The sky never looked so good to them as they walked to Earl's van.

"I'll take you both home," Earl said, starting the engine.

"We haven't eaten for what feels like days," Michael said.

Earl stopped at a Shell station a few miles away and bought them sandwiches and coffee. They ate in the back as he called Samantha, and handed Michael the phone. Then he called the Sheens' number. Felicity picked up and talked to Abby. Then Earl drove Abby to Richmond and took Michael to Kensington.

CHAPTER 80

Felicity was hugging a tearful Abby, Greg standing awkwardly in the hallway, as Earl took Michael to Kensington. The kiss Samantha gave him as he left didn't escape Michael's attention, but he didn't ask any questions. He enjoyed a long hot bath as Earl drove back to his garage to deal with Leonard Wells.

When he opened the garage door Leonard jumped him. He'd gotten his hands free, and cut the tape from his legs a few seconds before Earl arrived. Leonard got Earl in a choke. Earl threw him over his shoulder. Leonard got up and threw a punch, knocking Earl against the door.

Earl hit him hard, but Leonard smashed Earl in the face with his elbow. Then he head-butted him. Earl couldn't see for a few seconds. He felt blood on his face.

When he focused again Leonard was gone. Earl ran out of the garage, into the road, and saw his back, but he was sprinting too fast, and Earl was bleeding too hard to follow him.

Earl went back to Samantha, and she tended to him while Michael slept. Then she made them some pasta and opened a bottle of red wine.

"I told him about his father. He asked where he was. Poor boy is exhausted," she said.

"He isn't physically hurt, but psychologically he and Abby will need time to recover. Leonard Wells killed two people. I think Michael and Abby saw it. He left their bodies by their cages."

"Do you know who they are?"

"No idea. I want to speak to Michael about it when he's had some rest. Then I better call the police. The problem is that will open up an investigation into the whole kidnapping and we might look implicated."

"Thank you for finding Michael," she said, laying her hand on his shoulder.

"I did what I was hired to do."

She kissed him, taking his mouth with hers. He stayed the night. When he woke the next morning, Samantha was coming out of the bathroom naked. The arch of her back, the curve of her breasts, seemed the same as when they'd dated. And he wondered what their lives would have been like if he had married her.

CHAPTER 61

The teenagers Leonard had seen, when he left to meet his supposed client, had been hanging around outside the garages for some time. They returned later that night to shoot up. A passerby noticed them from the road and called the police. The teenagers were about to leave when they noticed the end garage was open.

Earl hadn't closed the door when he left with Michael and Abby.

The teenagers went in to see if there was anything worth stealing inside. They found the bathroom and the smashed door, and they found the ladder. They went down into the glass house. They saw the two bodies. They ran out of there, straight into two police officers.

When Leonard escaped, he walked all the way back to his garage, where he was arrested. He refused to say anything, but his prints were all over the place.

တသတ

Two days later, Micky Fallow was shot in a drive-by. He was leaving his favorite restaurant in London, smoking a Cuban cigar and thinking about all the things he was going to do to Samantha in bed, when an Audi raced past, and two bullets were fired from an open window. The hit man was sent by Jimmy Peach. He used hollow-point bullets for maximum damage.

Fallow was dead by the time he got to hospital. He had nothing on paper about his relationship with Julian Villa, and so what Julian had left that was free from debt was also free from the threat of Fallow.

Anne was a wealthy woman with Fallow gone. And Jimmy Peach continued to enjoy her as his favorite treat.

As Samantha tried to piece together the financial mess her husband had left her with, it became clear that the house was hers.

There was no claim on it, although Julian's offices and everything else he owned would go to the bank. Julian had taken a mortgage out on the house but it was still worth considerably more than the loan.

Samantha decided to sell it. She calculated that, when she'd paid the mortgage off and cleared some of the other debts Julian had left behind, she would have over two million.

CHAPTER 82

Abby was so relieved to be safe and with her family, she didn't pick up on the tension between her father and mother. Greg's guilt at what he'd done worsened now that he again saw the young woman he'd always felt was his daughter. One morning, Abby got up and heard raised voices. She went downstairs and listened to the row that was erupting between Felicity and Greg.

"How could you have done it?" Felicity said.

"Because of what you did with Julian."

"She is your daughter."

"Not biologically."

That was when Abby walked in. "What is going on?" she said.

"I'm sorry," Felicity said, throwing her arms around her as Greg poured himself another glass of Tesco brandy.

Felicity sat Abby down and told her about her parentage. She didn't tell her that Greg had hired Leonard Wells.

"But you still love me, don't you?" Abby said to Greg. "Otherwise, you wouldn't have tried to get me out of that place."

Greg's eyes pooled with tears as he held her in his arms. "Of course, I do. You're my daughter."

As Abby took a bath, Felicity took Greg to the bedroom. She undressed and, as he made love to her, her face was full of pleasure. She moaned softly as she came.

"Do you think we can put it all behind us?" she said afterward as they lay there.

"I want that. We should celebrate getting Abby back."

"Even with Tesco brandy?"

"I might be able to splash out on something a bit better. You know it's all been out of control for too long, first finding out about you, then Abby, then hiring that man. I really thought he going to kill her. I was so angry with you after I found out about you and Julian, I thought you'd lied about everything."

"I didn't lie about Abby. I didn't know."

"I realise that now."

CHAPTER 65

That afternoon, Michael had lunch with Samantha and Earl. He knew Earl had stayed the night and, as he enjoyed a cold beer, he noticed how relaxed his mother was. Abby had called him that morning and told him about her parentage. He'd spoken to Samantha about it. And, while it reignited her anger at Julian, her relief at having Michael back extinguished the fire.

"I can't believe my father was in so much debt," Michael said. "There's so much to take in, the fact that he's been murdered, the fact that Abby is my half-sister."

"I know," Samantha said, putting her hand on his.

"And by the way, I'm okay about you two."

"I'm glad."

"I know your marriage wasn't a happy one."

Later that day, Earl moved some things in. And Samantha instructed an estate agent to put the house on the market.

"What do you think has happened to Leonard Wells?" she said to Earl.

"That I don't know, but he doesn't have this address, and I don't think he'll be bothering us. What is concerning me are the two bodies I saw."

"Are you going to call the police?"

"I think I'll have to."

"You think they'll dig into the kidnapping?"

"It's likely. The problem is we've ignored them. They won't like that. I'll have to explain how I found the glass house, and I'll be a suspect. If I don't report it, it's morally worse. The problem is, the law is inept and so is policing."

"Do you think he'll go after Greg?"

"That's another matter."

Earl took Samantha into the bedroom and made love to her. Later that day, he put his flat on the market.

As it was, there was no need to make the call and jeopardise their fragile safety. Michael went to buy more beer that afternoon and returned with a copy of *The Times*. "He's been arrested. The police have found the glass house and the bodies."

Earl and Samantha read the article.

"He must have gone straight back there," Earl said.

"I'll phone Greg and let him know," Samantha said.

CHAPTER 64

It was all over the papers. The police identified the bodies of Pam Smythe and Francis Truman. They'd been reported missing by Pam's housemate and Truman's wife.

Leonard Wells didn't help his own case. When he was arrested, he attacked two police officers, breaking one of their noses. He refused to talk when interrogated. Over the ensuing months, Earl followed the coverage. There was no mention of a kidnapping, much to Greg's relief. Whether Leonard had spoken of it or not, remained unknown, but it seemed unlikely as there was no contact from the police. Finally, Leonard went to trial.

He was sentenced to life for the murders of Pam Smythe and Francis Truman. His torture and killing of two medical professionals shocked the public and angered the jury. The details of the strange prison made for good legal argument. But neither the lawyer for the prosecution nor the defense knew the real reason the glass house existed in the basement below a garage in a deserted area.

Leonard didn't give up the reason he'd built it. Like the garage where he'd worked out and tortured his victims, his decision not to talk about his motivation existed on two levels. Firstly, admitting to kidnapping, although he would take revenge by incriminating Greg, would add to his sentence. Secondly, he couldn't talk about why he'd built the glass house. It belonged in his dreams, or rather his nightmares, the ones he woke from screaming at night as he saw Kenny's butchered face.

It was a construction his mind had made, where he tortured the men he held responsible for Kenny's death and all the things he felt were wrong with British society. The glass house didn't exist for Leonard, except in his imagination. The torture of Abby and Michael, and the killing of Pam Smythe and Francis Truman seemed vague and unreal to him, as if he'd been acting under the influence of a drug.

The conclusion the jury reached was that he'd been keeping Pam Smythe and Francis Truman in the cages. The forensic evidence of burned tarantulas added to the profile of a serial killer. It also showed other people had been held prisoner. The prosecution lawyer put forward the theory that Leonard Wells had killed more people but he'd hidden the bodies.

Still, Leonard said nothing. When Harry visited him in prison, Leonard asked how Mandy was.

"We're giving it another go," Harry said.

"Yeah, well, you've got the dosh."

"Not everything's about money, Len. Things ain't as simple as that. You think I bought Mandy?"

"If it ain't about money, it's about class."

"No it ain't, you and I come from the same background."

"You beat her up?"

"No, I ain't beat her up. I was angry, wouldn't you be?"

"How's Mum?"

"She's all right, sends her love."

"I reckon I'll get out of here before long."

"Len, why did you do it?"

"Why do you think?"

"I know they neglected Mum, but to do that? And that place you took them to."

"I built it, plumbed it in, learned my trade from you, Harry."

"The glass house, where did you ever come up with that?"

"I've been living in it ever since Kenny died."

"I haven't let Mum read about it all, not everything they put in the papers."

"Yeah, well, you always did like to run the show."

"They ain't gonna let you out of here."

"Send my love to Mum."

Leonard signaled to a guard and left Harry sitting at the table with wet eyes. Leonard returned to his cell, where he sat on the edge of his bed, his stare locked on the wall, not seeing it, but the film of the war he fought every day.

ессо

Greg and Felicity began to enjoy married life again. Greg's strong sense of a paternal bond with Abby made him reassess the past. They put the house on the market and decided to clear as much of Greg's debt as possible with the proceeds before moving. Abby went on to pass her arts course. Michael took up photography and discovered he had a talent for it. His photographs began to win awards and were displayed in many leading magazines.

He lived with his mother and Earl at their new house in Kensington. It was a lot smaller, but with the sale of Earl's flat they managed fine. He saw Abby often and Samantha spoke to Greg and Felicity from time to time. They all read about the trial. But Michael and Abby chose minimum exposure, preferring to forget. Once Leonard Wells was put away, the memories of the ordeal he'd put them through began to fade.

Some months later, Leonard attacked a fellow prisoner. He'd somehow gotten hold of a long shard of glass, and he severed the prisoner's neck with it over lunch. Then he began to talk about the kidnapping, and how he'd been hired to do it. He mentioned Greg and Micky Fallow. But Fallow was dead, and Greg had Felicity's support.

Together, they denied all knowledge of Leonard Wells. But still the papers dug and, for a time, their lives were intruded on. Abby didn't know of the press interest, and they didn't tell her. And while they mentioned it to Samantha, she and Earl decided to leave it buried. The revelation of who hired the kidnapper would be too much for Abby and Michael.

And so they left Leonard Wells locked away. But they still thought about the glass house and what it meant. It seemed, finally, an image of fragility and the voyeurism and violence that fear of fragility can lead to. And when she thought about the past, Samantha felt she'd been living in a glass house for years with Julian, unable to see what was going on. With Earl, she had something back, and it was more than the past.

Eventually, Earl proposed to Samantha and she accepted.

They are happily married, and they guard their privacy as if it is a delicate wall around their lives.

About the Author

Richard Godwin is the critically acclaimed author of *Apostle Rising*, *Mr. Glamour*, *One Lost Summer*, *Noir City*, *Meaningful Conversations*, *Confessions Of A Hit Man*, *Paranoia And The Destiny Programme*, *Wrong Crowd*, *Savage Highway*, *Double Lives*, *The Pure And The Hated*, *Disembodied*, *Buffalo And Sour Mash* and *Locked In Cages*. His stories have been published in numerous paying magazines and over thirty-four anthologies, among them an anthology of his stories, *Piquant: Tales Of The Mustard Man*, *The Mammoth Book Of Best British Crime* and *The Mammoth Book Of Best British Mystery*, alongside Lee Child.

He was born in London and lectured in English and American literature at the University of London. He also teaches creative writing at University and workshops.

You can find out more about him at his website www.richardgodwin.net , where you can read a full list of his works, and where you can also read his *Chin Wags At The Slaughterhouse*, his highly popular and unusual interviews with other authors.